PAPER

The Dreams of A Scribe

BY THE SAME AUTHOR

THE SADDLEBAG

PAPER

The Dreams of A Scribe

Bahiyyih Nakhjavani

BLOOMSBURY

First published 2004

Copyright © 2004 by Bahiyyih Nakhjavani

The moral right of the author has been asserted.

Bloomsbury Publishing Plc, 38 Soho Square, London WID 3HB

A CIP catalogue record for this book
is available from the British Library.

ISBN 0 7475 6921 5

10 9 8 7 6 5 4 3 2 1

All papers used by Bloomsbury Publishing are natural, recyclable
products made from wood grown in well-managed forests.
The manufacturing processes conform to the
environmental regulations of the country of origin.

Typeset by Hewer Text Ltd, Edinburgh
Printed by Clays Ltd, St Ives Plc

CONTENTS

WOOD-PULP PAPER

SILK PAPER

SPIRIT PAPER

I prayse the man, that first did Paper make,
The onely thing that sets all virtues forth:
It shoes new bookes, and keeps old workes awake,
Much more of price that all this world is worth;
Though parchment duer, a greater time and space,
Yet can it not put paper out of place:
For paper still from man to man doth go,
When parchment comes in few men's hands, you
  knowe . . .

                              Thomas Churchyard

The fibrous substance called paper is regarded in a
vastly different light in the Orient from what it is in
the Occident, for in the Far East it has a spiritual
significance that overshadows its practical use, while
in the Western world the purposes for which paper is
intended are purely practical and utilitarian.

                              Dard Hunter

One might almost say that paper consists of a large
number of holes surrounded by fibres.

                              Helen Loveday

Paper is tenacious. It seems to survive censorship,
warfare, natural disasters and wastage better than
do human beings. Texts regarded as lost or wholly
forgotten turn up and not only in desert sands.

                              George Steiner

STRAW PAPER

To be classed as true paper the thin sheets must be made from fibres that have been macerated until each individual filament is a separate unit; the fibres inter-mixed with water, and by use of a sieve-like screen, the fibres lifted from the water in the form of a thin stratum, the water draining through the small openings of the screen leaving a sheet of matted fibre upon the screen's surface. This thin layer of intertwined fibre is paper.

Dard Hunter, 1943

THE FIRST DREAM

The Scribe was having a dream in his delirium.

He dreamed that he was walking in melting snow beside a river. He walked immaculate along a path, among clusters of hyacinths, between rows of conciliatory cypresses, and his feet were delicate as he trod. They were hyacinths of wisdom – ruby and amber and sapphire blue – and the cypresses were modest in their magnanimity. They dipped their heads above him as he walked, with an air of sovereign remedy. And he noted with a tincture of surprise that the waters of the river flowed with the sweet companionship of milk and the air hung pure as beaten silver all about him.

There was a bridge in his dream, which spanned the milky river like a chant, with its head to the east and its feet to the west. And as he approached it, he glimpsed a waiting orchard on the other side. It was an orchard full of cherry trees in bloom and the petals from the blossoms fell like pieces of paper all over the ground.

The Scribe was seized with a sense of urgency and excitement when he saw the orchard. The season would change; the paper would disintegrate! He had to gather it quickly. He had to gather it all! Without further reflection, he ran across the bridge to the harvest on the other side. He picked with his right hand and cradled the paper in his left, and the more he picked the more he was unable to resist from picking, for when paper is abundant and ink flows well, a scribe may naturally be inclined towards self-indulgence. The bundle of papers grew thick against his heart and his arms ached with anticipation.

Then suddenly, he saw someone sitting under a cherry tree before him. And instantly he knew that it was a poet. His words were sweet enough to attract the flies, but it was evident that the poet himself did not understand their full significance. He sat serene on a carpet in the middle of the orchard and contemplated the tree above him, his right hand hidden inside the green silk sleeve of his tunic and his left palm lying open on his knee. He made no effort to claim the paper, showed no interest in touching the edges or running his fingers along the surface to look for short cuts to perfection, but gazed up at the falling blossoms as if waiting for one sheet, the right sheet of paper, to drop into his hand. His face was aglow with patience and the Scribe understood that he had been waiting thus, with faith and without expectation, through countless seasons and for centuries.

The border of the carpet where the poet sat was clear to see, though it lay flat on the banks of the river, and its rectangular pattern struck the Scribe as unpleasantly familiar. He remembered this flatness; it made him obscurely ashamed. It was intended for the reader of perimeters who knew no more than was required of him. But the delicate petals floating down from the tree dissolved his discomfiture. They fell to the tune of tinkling camel bells and covered the carpet's designs from view. He felt immense gratitude towards the tree.

4

And then, with dawning wonder, the Scribe realized he was not only indebted to the tree but to the patience of the poet. As soon as he realized this, the load in his arms became as heavy as lead and all the paper he had gathered fell about him with a cascade of chimes.

*   *   *

The jingling of camel bells woke him. Somewhere, behind his head, beyond the wall of the mosque, below the steep slope of the rocky hillside and down along the dusty road that threaded through the valleys and across the violet mountain ridges of Persia, a camel train was coming to the eastern gates of the town. A caravan was approaching under the bright cerulean sky of the summer season, carrying rubies and fragrant ambergris, bringing luminous sheets of paper, perhaps. In his dawning consciousness, he heard the clang of the bells and the call of the camel drivers with a wonder bordering on new depths of delirium.

But his fever was broken. Although the sun was high and the heat of his room suffocating, he was alive and drenched in sweat, lying on his reed mats in a nest of dirty bedding. He stared, slightly puzzled, at the red Bokhara rug that hung before him. Then, as the dream dimmed, his muffled mind registered another sound from the road in the valley, below the mosque, behind the wall where his head was resting. It was the tramp of feet on rubble and stone, the harsh orders of an armed officer. A retinue of camels and a regiment of soldiers were marching through the gates. A prisoner was being conducted to the citadel high on the mountain passes of his memories, in this frontier town.

That was when he remembered his hand.

And at that moment, he forgot his dream entirely in his panic about his hand.

1 SUMMER

The Scribe styled himself a calligrapher and kept the nail on the thumb of his right hand filed conspicuously for this purpose. When reed pens were unavailable, or if he was to write poetry on especially smooth paper, he made a great show of dipping his thumb into the ink. The curious elongated nail, ending in a narrow, blackened wedge, compelled respect among the illiterate, demonstrated command over the written word. And respect of some kind had to be commanded among the rough Kurds in these mountains, even at the risk of infection. He did not have the right, shared by guard and prisoner alike, to enter the gates of the citadel; nor was he granted the grace by crown or chancery to cross the threshold of the palace. He was an itinerant copyist who earned his passage with paper and travelled on the strength of his pen: his right hand was his only mandate, his thumb his only mark of distinction.

No one knew what had brought the Scribe to this backwater the previous spring. The Mullah down at the mosque in town assumed that he was a disgraced cleric, hounded to remote frontiers by the taint of heresy. The Warden up at the citadel believed he was a disappointed scholar who had fled from the royal workshops in the northern capital when interpolations were discovered in the classic *Book of Kings*. A Russian surveyor in town was told that the taciturn amanuensis had been employed to entertain the dying Shah with the history of China and had received a trifling sum for his pains. But whatever the truth of the matter, everyone agreed that some catastrophe must have led him to this no-man's-land between uncertain empires.

It was a place between places at a time between times; it was an uncharted border between shifting regions and religions. Persia to the south and east was governed by a Shi'ia dynasty; Turkey to the west lay under the Sunni Sultanate; Armenia and Georgia, too, between the Black Sea and the Caspian in the north, maintained opposing claims and rival churches. In recent years, Cossacks who defended the interests of Mother Russia had begun to patrol the Southern Line, and English spies had been noticed fording the Aras and the Oxus. Internal enemies also festered on these frontiers. The ancient citadel, once a fortress against warring tribes, now contained rebels and notorious heretics. And depending on the season, Khans of opposing Marches controlled the pass above the town. If the Kurds still kept some measure of their freedom in these mountains, it was only because they quarrelled so much among themselves that no one could control them, in the Scribe's opinion.

He did not, however, share this opinion with anyone else, for a scribe had best keep his own counsel. Copyists were despised these days and fine calligraphers were under-valued; print had grown dismally popular among the merchant classes and lithography proliferated up and down the land. Sovereign manuscripts had been unbound, their gold and azure pages scattered to the wind, and the Crown

Prince himself had even patronized the use of wax to print the classics. As a result of such depredations, those who traded in the written word were growing redundant. With pen-cases in their belts and desks under their arms, men like the Scribe were forced to take refuge in the last havens of illiteracy. They had begun to wander through the highways and byways of the kingdom, begging shamelessly for paper.

For as the scribal bonds between books and men began to break, Persia had become paperless. As masters grew rare and their apprentices more reckless, the ancient Chinese arts were being forgotten. Gone were the lime vats of the old workshops, the reed moulds and the couching felts clogged with flies. Gone the tubs to steep the straw, the hammers to pulp the rags to pieces and the press to squeeze the paper dry. Even the local manufactory built near the capital a few years earlier had failed, due to the increase in British trade, and the only paper worthy of the name now came from foreign parts. Small wonder that the Scribe had turned his steps towards the border crossings and was wandering in the wake of passing caravans.

He was a queer fish, though, to be cast ashore beneath the land-locked peaks of Ararat; he was an odd traveller among the spies and traders en route between Tiflis and Trebizond, Erevan and Astrabad. No one expected him to stay long on these borders, for he had reached that age when a man sees he has done nothing and moves on because he has everything left to do. His peaked features and thick-fringed lashes did not at first glance betray him, but there was a darkness under his skin when he flushed which perturbed those who noticed, and although he was as thin as a reed, his lips had a full, bruised look that stirred the senses. They murmured in the coffeehouse that his

blood was made of ink, that he practised illicit vices, but
their doubts were soon forgotten when his services were
required. They called him Aqa Katib, to accredit him with
penmanship rather than a name, but whoever his master
was or might have been, his nail left an indelible mark on
those who met him.

The Scribe's nail was legendary among the townsfolk.
The thread of ink that spread from its tip widened the
ripples of awe around him. But it was paper rather than
pride that made him cherish this symbol of his profession.
He was obsessed with paper, possessed by it. His nail,
moving across the surface of the page, touched untold
passions, released unnamed desires. The thin whisper of
its scratching sound as he pressed down, the quiver of its tip
as it gave way beneath the pressure, the sudden run of jet-
black ink, stroke after irresistible stroke, as he caressed the
page, caused his heart to beat thick and fast and the blood
to hammer in his veins. He was a paper fanatic.

But his nail had become infected earlier that summer.
His hand had bloated, the skin tight as a sheep's bladder
filled with yoghurt, and he had fallen sick with a zymotic
fever. It was too late to lance the thumb but had they cut
off his hand –?

The camel bells jingled in his ears as he tried to lift his hand
but it was pinioned down like lead. The tramp of feet beat in
his head as he tried to see if the ooze of pus had eaten the
bone, if the obscene swelling had become a bloody stump,
like the hand of the beggar at the coffee-house, like a piece of
meat the butchers wrapped in rough hemp papers. But he
could only turn towards the light, and moan.

The stained Bokhara rug which divided the Scribe's
room was drawn aside and a towering figure blocked the
summer dazzle of the door.

'He lives!' bellowed this apparition.

The loud voice grated like chalk against the slate of the Scribe's weak consciousness. His mind surfaced slowly, saturated with sleep, limp on the mesh of dreams as another presence barrelled into his room. Immortality was congested.

'It's a miracle!' blinked the old man who had entered. 'Or a catastrophe,' he added doubtfully. This was the Mullah who had given the Scribe refuge in the mosque when he first came to these mountains. It was the melancholy cleric to whom he had offered his secretarial services in lieu of rent. The pain in his wrist was a reminder that every single sheet of straw paper lying like a thick mattress under his tumbled bedding was destined for the Mullah's endless will. Despite this fact, the Scribe was comforted by covenants of recollection at the sight of him and risked a smile. But he winced as the third member of the seraphic host squeezed into his crowded paradise. She was buckled with the exertions of faith and arthritis and her arms dripped suds from the elbows down, like a pair of laundered wings. When she saw the Scribe, she fluttered her featherless hands in a last surrender to certitude.

'Aqa Katib isn't dead after all!' she shrilled, as if he could deny it.

The Scribe surfaced with a jolt. His dream had drained away entirely and he lay drying under the pressure of the three pairs of eyes. The third presence was the Widow, he remembered, a faithful servant of the Mullah whose prayers bobbed over the surface of her limpid soul, like chicks across the dust. A true believer, she had prayed earnestly for his recovery when his hand became infected but it had been all in vain. Somewhat deaf, she leaned on other people's conversations to make up for her heaviness of hearing, but the Scribe could still not identify who supported her.

'A new age has dawned!' boomed this apparition again. 'The Healer of the People has performed another miracle!' And to prove it, he pulled aside the carpet from the beams above the bed, and sunlight flooded into the Scribe's back room.

This carpet, which divided the Scribe's sleeping quarters from his workshop, was not the exuberant kind covered in garden imagery anticipating paradise, nor a prayer mat, aspiring to precarious states of spiritual equilibrium. Marred by a stain too large to be rust and too red to be innocent, it was a reminder, merely, of the decorum required to conceal the squalor of daily life, the complacence needed to ignore its banal violences. It contrived to hide reality from view and when it was pulled aside, the Scribe felt all his hypocrisies exposed before the blazing door. As the rug fell from the beams above him, bringing a shower of wattle and daub and plaster and several surprised lizards down on the company of the righteous, he raised his right arm to protect himself from shame, wrenching it free with a howl of pain.

There was an uproar as a jumble of ropes and pulleys and funnels and pipes and two large sunbaked bricks crashed down with the carpet. And as the debris scattered over the prostrate Scribe, he saw his hand was intact: it was wrapped in paper but the swelling was gone, the thumb whole, the blackened nail no longer infected. That was when he remembered who had thrown lizards and shame upon him. Healer of the people indeed! It was the quack from the Caucasus! It was the Charlatan who controlled his supplies and held him hostage to straw paper!

He pulled himself, trembling, against the wall and shook

a miraculous fist at the loud man who towered over the dust and wreckage of his room.

'Get out of here!' he spat, his voice thin with rage.

The Mullah gaped, the Charlatan stared, the Widow could hardly believe her ears: the Scribe was a man of few words, and they were generally confined to the page. But he was tearing the paper wrapping off his hand, in a blind fury.

'Get out and take your rotten talismans with you!' hissed the risen corpse.

For a moment, the lizards were immobilized, and then they were swept off the quilts by the Charlatan's hurt pride. He could not endure insults to his profession.

'Ingrate!' he roared. 'I cured your hand and is this all your thanks? To the devil with you and be damned! Who needs a common scribbler anyway? From this time forth, the Healer of the People shall rely on the reverends of Philadelphia and the printed word!'

And with that bolt, he stormed out of the mosque, relegating the scribal arts to obsolescence and calling dry ink-wells and catastrophe upon the house. The Widow shrieked at his predictions and the Mullah lumbered after the walking oracle, shaking his head in sorrow. But the Charlatan's wrath was implacable. 'And don't think you'll get any more straw from me!' he hollered from the court-yard. And turning his back on them all, he rattled down the sloping path to the southern gates of the town.

As the voice of the Charlatan was buried under an avalanche of pebbles, the Scribe sank back on his dusty quilts, blanched and trembling. He was unaccustomed to the force of his own words. But it was only after the evening curfew marked the closing of the gates, it was only as the fruit bats surged into the fig tree, and the Mullah subsided in the twilight of his water-pipe, that their full impact hit him. Leaning against the pockmarked walls of his ruined room, he suddenly realized that he had given up his sole supply of paper. He had deprived himself of his livelihood. He had lost his only chance of sanctuary. Without paper, he was nothing.

The tottering straw heaped in his room and the reams stacked beneath his mattresses were his last bulwark, his only defence against the dusty road that sloped down the rose-tinted mountain, that meandered through the purple valleys and the twilight plains of Persia, that wound its inexorable way into dim and umber distances behind his head.

2 A HOT NIGHT

T hat night, after the Charlatan's departure, the Scribe
lay half-asleep and half-awake, counting sheets of
paper between the Widow's snores. Their sonorous surfaces did not betray much, but when history's face is scored
by wrinkles, it surpasses the need for a veil. The old woman
had devoted so many years to the melancholy cleric that
whoever her dead husband might have been, her memories
of him could not have been so bountiful, for her snores
were heavy with relief.

The Scribe and the Mullah occupied facing rooms on
opposite sides of the mosque. Between their doors across
the courtyard was the northern entrance to the building,
which travellers used when they took shelter for the night,
behind the pulpit. But in summer, when everyone slept on
the roof to escape the heat, the hot courtyard belonged to
the Widow who filled the darkness with her sighs and
snores.

Due to his fever, the Scribe was confined to his room
that night and tossed about in the prickly heat, his paper
mattress covered with dream dust, his pillows gritty with
anxiety. Each time he drifted off, he thought he was
dropping paper all over the ground; each time he dozed,

he imagined he was scrambling on his hands and knees to pick the pieces from the floor. The season would pass, he thought in a panic. The pieces would perish! He had to save the paper to write the poem of his dreams. Because when the catastrophe of his hand was averted, the Scribe knew that the time of miracles had come. When the Prisoner arrived at the turning of the summer season, he began to believe that his hand had been saved so that he might be a poet.

*   *   *

Although he was a pen-pusher by day, the Scribe exercised less public arts at night. He practised his calligraphy secretly, by lamplight. He refined his five grades of writing from the nineteen styles prescribed, and struggled on the lonely privacy of the page to perfect his thousand lines of life, as was expected of one who wanted to be more than a mere copyist. He had always wanted to be more than a mere copyist. He yearned to write words no one dictated, to become a poet.

But he had never possessed the paper to fulfil his dreams.

When he first arrived at these frontiers the Scribe received a single ream of paper when the trade caravans from the south passed through the valley of Darreh Sham. Although it never satisfied his longings, this paper was the way he earned his living. He used it to acquire goat's cheese from widows waiting to hear from long-lost sons, dried fruits from peasants with rich relatives in far-off towns, and tea, if replies ever arrived from anyone. When they did not, he usually found extenuating circumstances buried in a page, for a handful of nuts. Besides, the formula for official documents was always the same. Jute offered as much assurance of justice as the finest paper in the land and

15

so it was sufficient to give praise to God in the first paragraph, name sons in the second, and make respectful mention of a score of goats or a daughter in the third. He recorded contracts for a leg of lamb and when the brittle paper cracked, he copied them for a bushel of hot plums. Straw paper kept him alive.

But it was not conducive to the writing of poetry. The stuff was made of insults and macerated hemp; it tugged irritatingly at the tip of the pen, forming unsightly blots at every line. It was as porous as the Widow's nose and could not resist the bite of his reed. It caused his inks to lose their lustre and sink into the surface like spittle in sand. The carbon drained too quickly and the carmine ran. But there was no alternative. For the Scribe's paper-making days had passed with his apprenticeship and since he had taken to the roads, he no longer practised his craft. Who could drain the matted tissue on the backs of mules, or travel with the weights to press them down? And where were the brothers in the trade, to slap the clinging sheets against dry walls for him, to hang them, moist and without wrinkling, on the lines? True paper needed time and place and fellowship to be well made. And since he had none of these, he had to scrounge whatever reams he could, polish them the best that he was able, and size them with the cheapest paste he found along his way.

Far from having a place to make paper, it was only when the Scribe had paper that he could stay in one place. But he needed a substantial stockpile if he was to remain at these frontiers, for his landlord's codicils piled upon one side of the building faster than the straw could accumulate on the other. Butchers would have been eager to buy his surplus, for though the surface was too rough for ink, its absorbent qualities were excellent for blood. Gamblers in the coffeehouse would have been glad to relieve him of it too, because the paper disintegrated easily and was ideal for promissory notes. But the Mullah's will required more than could be soaked up by all the blood and debts in the region. Even the Russian surveyor could not compel him to sell more than a few sheets for the laissez-passer authorizing him to leave the town, for these reams were all that permitted the Scribe himself to stay. In fact, it was to keep the roof over his head that he established a paper partnership with the Charlatan.

A middleman for the Greek traders between Tabriz and Trebizond, the Charlatan came to the town each week to sell needles and soap to the townsfolk.

'Sweet as the girl in your dreams!' he would bellow to the Kurds, deluding them with slippery associations between soap and chastity. 'Sharp as your minds!' he promised the housewives, sliding a needle in the skin between his forefinger and thumb. Then he blew on the needle, pretended to hammer it into his head, and finally appeared to pluck it out of the back of his head. They were ravished.

He also sold straw paper to the Scribe, as a special bonus.

'It'll wrap your heart in poetry!' he boomed across the bazaar.

The Scribe had been deprived of higher forms of flattery for a long time.

'It soaks up sorrows and turns them to smiles,' glozed the Charlatan.

But the stuff was totally unusable.

The Charlatan turned his attentions elsewhere. 'Wear it in your shoes and walk to eternity!' he cried to the Mullah. 'Write your prayers with every step!' he bellowed. He had a shrewd perception of his audience, and the Mullah, whose gout was a severe impediment to his gait, lingered to listen to him. 'Words change but the paper doesn't!' cried the quack. 'Pens may be different but the paper's one! Look!' he said, poking a hole through a piece. 'It's all the same under the ink, my friends!' And he threw the paper into the air, to the intense excitement of the street urchins.

The cleric had been much struck by the quack's claims. Could paper unite people, he wondered; could it bring together Kurd and Christian, Jew and Turk? Pages of the Quran and the Avestas, copies of the Orthodox and Apostolic Testaments, both old and new, had drifted across these mountains since the ebbing of the Flood, but these had divided rather than reconciled the inhabitants of the region. The mosque itself, over which the Mullah presided, stood outside the town because of its associations with the Shi'ia minority in this Sunni region, and this conundrum caused the Mullah many sleepless nights. He was much exercised by the singleness of God in the face of His multiple Holy Books. Could paper provide the common ground of understanding between them? Was this the mystic oneness underlying all words?

Despite the quack's compelling oratory, the Mullah's literal-mindedness was orthodox. Blank paper could soak up heresies too, he reminded himself; it could absorb falsehood as indiscriminately as truth. In his youth he had indulged in certain heretical theories, which invited him to consider the futility of his role in society, the abdication of his rank, and so he wanted to make sure of God's grammar before he died. He was determined to write his will and testament according to divine syntax. All chance accidents and unexpected reprieves – the arrival of a stained carpet on his step, the departure of a visitor from his doors – were interpreted according to this lexicon. Even the most trivial occurrences – the falling of a ladder, the greed of a goat – could be read in the light of this glossary. He wanted to note every deviation from the rule, parse each pause of moral impulse, analyse each lapse of conscience before he died. For the inflection placed on the syllable of an act, in his opinion, made all the difference to its meaning. But despite his best efforts, there appeared to be inscrutable gaps in God's logic; despite all his care, heresies continued to glint between the lines. His will had thus become subject to repeated qualifications and ramifications. In the context of the booming bazaar, it was disturbing to contemplate that God might prefer his silences.

'It's a substitute for courage, I'm telling you!' hollered the paper salesman. 'All you need is paper and a prayer and you can face the Turkmen with your chest hairs bare! As urgent as trousers, as subtle as the veil!' he continued, with a bright eye on the fluttering women at the edge of the crowd. 'And as necessary as soap! See this froth, ladies and gentlemen? The very best in town!'

He had a strong voice, mellow as autumn honey, and a special way with women. They murmured that he had wives all over the Caucasus and had gone on pilgrimage to Europe, for he made seductive references to western capitals and claimed that scientific progress fulfilled religious prophecy. Small wonder that the Widow returned from the bazaar laden with soap and praise. She never questioned what lay behind words as long as she could hear them. The Charlatan's soap was as good as a prayer to her and she cleansed the mosque with it five times a day.

'You should listen to him talk,' she reported breathlessly. 'Frothed up everything, just like he promised! He's a regular prophet for lather,' she concluded.

The Scribe was not convinced. Poetry needed no advertisement, in his opinion.

But it was not long before the Charlatan's soap began to

acquire curative powers and the Scribe gradually complained less about his paper. They had come to an agreement, apparently. The Charlatan provided the Scribe with supplies and he wrote holy verses for the quack in exchange. He scribbled talismans on teacups, under soles of shoes, folded into hems of robes and tucked inside the bands wound round the shaven heads of schoolboys infested with lice. He wrote amulets for convoluted tubes intended to relieve constipation, for eye pumps, which had stimulating powers that extended to the organs of generation, and for a travelling womb, the secret of whose success lay in the holy paper rolled inside it. The Charlatan's homeopathy of pulp was suited to each need, appropriate for each time. Melancholy songbirds could be transformed to nightingales on paper; flies could be vanquished and donkeys protected with paper. Since it was porous, it could soak up vice and protect virtue, the Charlatan said: antidotes for living could be acquired by laying it on graves of the dead. He also prescribed paper cures in doubtful cases of pre-nuptial chastity. Since virginity was as uncertain as the paper fragile, however, none of the Charlatan's dictates had thus far transformed the Scribe into a poet.

According to the Mullah, poets did not possess the keys of immortality. They were not, technically speaking, accounted among the faithful or given rights of access to those paradisiacal fairies possessed of elastic chastity. And to imagine otherwise bordered on heresy, in his opinion. But the Scribe had seen black-eyed houris peeping from behind the jewelled surfaces of miniatures; he had read, in the traditions, that poets could sometimes unlock untold treasures beneath the throne of God. Even if the keys to paradise were out of the question, he harboured private dreams of fingering the spiritual dust accumulated beneath such articles of divine furniture. He wanted to probe those impenetrable recesses, reach that tender place between the words.

In youth, he had written several vapid odes in praise of this uncertain theme; he had composed love letters, which had liberated his thumb gratifyingly. There had been a time when a glimpse of his master's daughter, looking down through the dust motes of the workshop, could cause him to lose all perspective, when the sight of a curl against her glancing cheek could flatten his mind. But despite these memories glimmering like pale moths behind the fretwork of the years, no poems had been forthcoming. He had scanned his polished pages, but the grace of self-forgetfulness had not returned. And although his paper-partnership provided him with the illusion of security, his thumb had sickened since his coming to this town.

*   *   *

Some time in the middle of the night, the Scribe was roused from his fitful slumbers by voices. The Mullah sounded loud outside his door.

'It's hopeless,' he was saying. 'They'll never let you in!'

The Scribe assumed the cleric was shouting in his sleep, for he often conducted nocturnal arguments with the angels at the gates of paradise. Since the Widow's snores continued unperturbed despite these dire warnings, he assumed that the celestial sentinels were obdurate. But other sounds soon intervened. It seemed to him that there were unloadings in the stables, lumberings across the courtyard, breathings behind the pulpit of the mosque. Between the turning pages of the Widow's snores, he thought he heard rustlings, foldings, tearings and crumplings around him. Either jinns were carting loads of paper from heaven into hell, he thought, or else a traveller had arrived.

At that thought, all further prospects of sleep were banished for the Scribe. He lay wide awake counting imaginary pieces fluttering from his room to the Mullah's, on the other side of the courtyard. It occurred to him that as the weight of paper tipped the balance of the mosque, his life too would pitch and toss on the rocky outcrop. But he never considered that its equilibrium could depend on the Widow in the courtyard between them. He did not associate poetry with snoring.

The old woman snored steadily under the fig tree, her head to the east and her feet to the west. She snored serenely, and with the milky dawn, she rolled up her mats, rose to her creaking feet and mumbled her grateful prayers with the birds. Her own dreams had been unmemorable that night and rendered nothing to the dawn but an empty bucket from the well to make the morning tea. But the strident cheeping from the stables confirmed catastrophes, for the well was dry and there was a drought.

3 CATASTROPHES

As the cock heralded the sun, there was a crash and a thud in the stables. The Widow invariably caused the ladder to fall when she greeted her chickens in the rafters, but this morning her usual protestations rose to a crescendo when she found three baby chicks lying with their horny feet curled up and their beaks agape in the straw. Floods of tears could not revive them or fill the empty well.

'The catastrophe has come!' she lamented. For in addition to the drought, the ragged Bokhara, relegated to the courtyard the previous night, had served as breakfast for the insolent goat. 'His predictions have come true!' she wailed, holding up a mangled corner in evidence of the Charlatan's fatidical powers. It was the worst of omens. When a carpet is chewed by a goat, what is to stop the world's order from being rolled up and cast aside for ever?

The Scribe swayed under the eaves, gritting his teeth to steady himself. The Charlatan's bombast was unfortunately rooted in reality. For his recent visits to the south were connected with some missionaries on the shores of the Salt Lake who were printing bibles for the betterment of their Nestorian flock. This was even worse than the threat of lithographic presses in Tabriz and faraway Teheran, for the monstrous machines from Philadelphia had an insatiable appetite and devoured reams automatically. It was one thing to reject a humiliating partnership with the Charlatan and quite another to know that Presbyterians would benefit from his loss. It was unthinkable for the Scribe that the fulfilment of his dreams and the writing of his poems should have coincided with a season of drought and dwindling paper.

The Mullah read anguish on his secretary's face and instructed the Widow to avoid all further mention of catastrophe that morning. He also exercised rare circumspection himself and did not say a word about his dream. For after installing a late traveller in the mosque the previous night, the Mullah had lain beneath the stars and drifted into a deep slumber. A melancholy insomniac with a tendency to gout, the old man generally slept little and lightly, but that night he had dreamed it was the first day of the world. He dreamed, moreover, that the Scribe had been told to record the book of creation for posterity, and to his dismay there was no space left in it for his will. The Scribe had smudged all the margins of life; he had left smears across the land, and sullied all the seas with ink. Since only blank paper could ensure against heresy, the old man was much exercised, in his dream, by an urge to wash this ink away.

Although creation was normally interpreted in the past tense, the Mullah's dream must have been conjugated with the future in mind, because the tea tasted of lamp soot and gall that morning. The sight of his secretary's drawn face against the wall, however, concentrated his thoughts on prevention rather than premonition, and so he permitted the Widow to hang pages of his will on the fig tree, to forestall the death of chickens and protect the household against covetousness.

It can't replenish my paper supply though, thought the Scribe glumly, but he accepted the invitation to sit on the

chewed corners of the old world order and eat some breakfast with his host. He choked on the inky tea, however, and
could barely swallow the pulpy bread. Paper thickened his
tongue and filled his throat and rasped under his eyelids; it
was stuffed in his ears too, as the Mullah's testament
soughed in the branches overhead, like leaves from the
multiple seasons, like trees in the illumined miniatures of
paradise. This world and the next were made of paper,
concluded the Scribe dismally, and none of it was his.

But who had arrived so late the previous night?

Travellers of different persuasions passed this way, and
no matter what the hour, the kindly Mullah always gave
them hospitality. The only other room available in town
was at the coffeehouse, a place notorious for its fleas and
catamites, but the Mullah hoped that if people were united
in the common oblivion of sleep beneath his roof, they
might grow tolerant of one another. It seemed that the new
visitor barely slept at all, however. He was a Sufi from the
south, who had walked all the way to these northern
frontiers from the port of Bushire, to deliver his provisions
to the Prisoner. After piling his baggage behind the pulpit,
he had insisted on continuing up to the citadel at dawn.

'I told him the Warden has denied access to all visitors,'
said the Mullah sadly. 'But he was determined to request
for permission!'

The visitor had left the mosque as soon as the gates were
opened and only planned to return by evening. The Mullah
thought he would be lucky if he survived the day. The cleric
respected the mendicant orders for their worldly detachment but despised them for their lack of common sense. This
wandering Sufi was either suffering from delusions, or the
grace of God, he told the Scribe. For he had endured the
most fearful adventures on his way; he had witnessed won-

ders and been blessed with visions. He had seen the high passes covered in shimmering glass, apparently, as dazzling as the sun. But on closer questioning, it appeared that these marvels may have been caused by a major disaster. A consignment of mirrors had recently broken to smithereens on the trade route from Trebizond and the Mullah anticipated that the Warden's patience would be limited at such a time as this. When the odds were so heavily stacked against one, was it stupidity or faith to believe in an uncertain cause? The Mullah was curious to observe an exception of certitude to the general rules of doubt, but it did seem like heresy to pray for chickens, in the circumstances.

The Widow was disappointed and vented her frustrations on the goat.

'Confound your udders!' she cried, pumping hard at the poor creature as she squatted beside it. 'My chicks will die unless the Prisoner writes the drought away.'

The Scribe stared at her vacantly. 'Writes the drought –?' he repeated.

'He writes everything away,' nodded the Widow with another vindictive jerk.

The Scribe's world was erased in the pause that ensued.

'He can write a thousand verses in five hours,' she hazed, pumping ruthlessly.

He must have a great deal of paper in that case, thought the Scribe. Everything, in the end, boiled down to paper.

'And, what's more, he does it without stopping,' the Widow continued with a knowing wink.

The Scribe cleared his throat. 'What,' he brought out, 'does he write on?'

The Widow did not hear him. 'God dictates to him,' she explained helpfully, for she had been harvesting caravan gossip from the guards that morning. Divine dictation took the form of erasure, apparently: dearth, death, and even debt could be eradicated, as could despair and doubt. 'He can write anything away, as long as God dictates. He wrote the Shah off. He wrote off the Prime Minister too and several divines. And one night he almost wrote himself to the capital! That must take some doing!' she nodded. Her expertise on the subject was breathtaking.

'How much paper does it take for a drought?' rasped the Scribe.

The old woman had not considered this question. She struggled with the overwhelming nature of its mathematics, but finally concluded that it would probably take the Prisoner more paper to write off an epidemic, God forbid, than to stave a drought.

Although the goat escaped her fingers at this pious reflex, the Widow did not dwell on divine paradox for long. She was impervious to the cause when the effects of catastrophe claimed immediate attention. Since there was no alternative but the water-carriers, she rustled off to knot her headbands in preparation for the bazaar, for she faced the public street wrapped in cloth from head to foot, in the same way she anticipated being dead. Water was essential, from whatever source, she said.

The Scribe would have been willing to accept paper from any source too.

The Mullah noted the pallor of his skin and ordered him to rest for the day, to recuperate his strength. 'God may dictate but my will can wait,' he said kindly.

A few leaves spiralled from the fig tree as the Scribe rose to his feet. Swallows twittered under the eaves of his heart and the air seemed to tighten around him when he attempted to walk across the courtyard. He was exhausted by this Prisoner's prolixity. How could someone erase a drought, he thought, or write a flood without drowning? What calligra-phy could capture and quench fire, which script resist earthquakes or inflicted plagues? And where, above all, were the volumes that could contain such miracles and catastrophes, the quires which could be used yet remain unstained, the reams where words might shimmer without a stroke of ink being written down? If it existed, that was the paper of his dreams, the paper for his poem!

He shuffled slowly out of the shade of the fig tree, tasting the tannin of resentment on his tongue. He shuddered at the sight of the coarse straw paper tucked inside the Mullah's shoes and closed his eyes at the first blow of the blinding sun. He spat at a chicken that had wandered under his feet and sent it flapping across the dusty squalor of the courtyard; he cradled his wrist in the sleeve of his cotton shift as he approached his door. And then, as he leaned against the northern wall to catch his breath before groping over the threshold, he noticed, through the open doorway leading into the mosque, two large sacks in the gloom behind the pulpit. They must belong to the perambulating lunatic, he thought, and his wrist ached at their heaviness.

His hand had been badly strained by the Charlatan's contraption. In fact it was a wonder his thumb had not broken under the weight of all that science and progress. Unlike the Widow, who fervently believed the Charlatan to have cured him, the Scribe was certain that his quackery had been the cause of the infection in the first place. If a scribe's work was sloppy, filled with orthographical errors, stained with smears, rendered in a derivative script, blotted by poor penmanship and breathless with lack of space, it was probably because he served a charlatan. But he shuddered at the thought of refining his skills now that his source of paper was lost. Even if his hand had been saved, miracles might have a cost.

4 WRITING

After the Widow left for the bazaar, the Scribe wavered at the door of his room, irresolute. The indentations of the reed mat where he had been lying for the past few days had left ribbed chain lines on the surface of his thighs. He ran his fingertips across the furrows of his skin and pondered his future. A scribe without paper was like a fish without water, he thought, half-tempted to write on himself.

He settled his tools on a rush mat by the courtyard entrance, and leaned his head limply back in the shade of the stable eaves to gaze at the ominous cliff of Kizil Dagh. Cradling his bruised wrist in his sleeve and waiting for his strength to revive as the morning warmed, he watched the mountain road turn from glimmering grey to glowing pink and gleaming white before him.

There were three sets of gates through which the chalky road passed down the mountain. The first of these were the heavy iron-studded gates of the towered citadel itself, high above him. The rocks on which this fortress had been built were stained with fratricidal feuds from the time of Tamerlane. The citadel had witnessed fruitless strifes and ruinous wars for centuries and since the vein of ancient rivalries ran deep, it now served as a penitentiary for those who threatened the state. The Scribe shivered slightly at the thought of the Prisoner, scribbling his erasures overhead.

Just below it stood the gates of the Warden's residence, built on a ledge of rock under the citadel. The grandest building in the town, it was encircled by a whitewashed wall and stunted cypress trees, and was the seat from which the Khan of the Eastern Marches controlled his garrisons. The Kurdish troops were the backbone of the Persian army, but their loyalty could not be taken for granted in these shifting times. The Shah lay sick in the capital and everyone knew that once he died, the troops would be under a different command. It was hardly to be wondered that the Khan's authority had diminished in recent months. The Scribe thought he heard a melancholy note in the faint shouts of the soldiers being drilled that morning.

Below the palace and beneath the hidden moon, the road disappeared into the labyrinthine town itself. A huddle of sun-baked houses had been constructed pell-mell on the limestone slopes of a deep gorge, and the mosque of this cluttered little town, where the Scribe had taken refuge, was built on a slight promontory outside its southern gates, which closed at sunset and opened at dawn. Once through them, the road angled down the last incline of the mountain to cross the river at the toll bridge. When the Scribe looked below him, he could see it bending round the river by the post house before twisting through the torpid fields into the dusty violet distance. In spring the road was flooded like a river but in summer, when the vacant terraces were nibbled bare by goats and expectation, the riverbed became a second road. When there was drought or plague or flood or famine, however, travellers were confined to the caravanserai in the valley.

At such times there was always a paper crisis and a run on the couriers. For the strategic significance of these mountains had become apparent during the last decade's ignominious wars, when Russian troops had pushed to the very banks of the river Aras, rousing the warlords in the Caucasus, creating tensions among foreign envoys, and sending spies scuttling to both sides of the Caspian. Recently, due to millennial fervour along these frontiers, the Tsar's demands for security had grown particularly querulous. As a result, tension on these borders had increased and the town at the crossroads had acquired a cartographical importance that far belied its squalid appearance. There were seasonal flurries of paper in its narrow alleys which competed with snowstorms in their severity and the couriers made a killing.

The Scribe stared down at the road meandering through the valley, thinking of couriers streaking like dust storms from these frontiers, imagining letters and dispatches and messages whirling to the heart of the kingdom from these remote borders. For a moment, he thought he saw a paper road before him, scribbled by copyists, scrawled by scribes, fluttering like an unwinding ribbon under the sun. They were lost and scattered to the winds, those brief companions; they were gone now, but the road of paper still wound on. He blinked and rubbed his eyes.

There was no sign of life on the road today. No guards played dice along the parapet of the bridge, waiting to extract tolls. No couriers walked up the hillside, reeking of sweat and urgency. The dry gorge and the blistered pebbles only betrayed the lack of rains that month, the dust in his throat admitted loneliness. In the old days, copyists used to flee from catastrophes in search of new masters. But in more recent times, catastrophes stalked the kingdom, chasing scribes from place to place. There was nowhere to run to now. His circle had been broken; his masters were dead and his loves undone. The old world had passed and there was no sign of a new one.

The Scribe turned from the disconsolate sight of the poplars bordering the road and shifted closer to his pot of basil, to comfort himself. The Widow planted her kitchen herbs beneath the eaves, but the Scribe kept his basil in the shadow of his room, to preserve its fragrance. It had dried during his illness and only one leaf remained. He drew his hand tentatively from his sleeve and stretched it towards the pot. Then, nipping the basil leaf between his index and thumb, he lifted the heady odour to his nostrils and breathed. The leaf conveyed the relish of no pain, the ecstasy of immemorial forgiveness; it was a perfume laden with memories of the most Holy Book. It reminded him of the poet in the orchard, his palm lying open, so certain of paper, so generous in patience. As his parched lungs filled with it and his head spun, he had an absurd desire to throw himself down and kiss the imprint of his dream left there on the riverbank.

'I must write my poem on the finest paper in the land,' thought the Scribe unsteadily. 'It deserves a page as pure as a mirror, as eternal as a palm.'

And he stared down at his tools, his eyes brimming. If he wanted to command them again, he had to decipher the meaning of his hand. A scribe should know what he was writing with, from the curve of his thumb to the tips of his fingers, one by one. Brushing away his tears, he groped blindly for his burnisher, with his index.

He had used it since his student days. The tool was

invaluable to flatten the snarls and smooth the lumps in the cheap straw. Originally a glass stopper, it consisted of a smooth sphere that reflected mysterious reversals of the world within itself. The Scribe had thickened the base with clay and lengthened its handle for greater ease, but as he tried to pick it up that morning, its heaviness astonished him and his wrist began to ache unbearably. Paper had to be smooth enough to mirror the words with fidelity, but to press his index finger against this glass required more effort or integrity than he could muster now. After rubbing the burnisher back and forth laboriously for a few moments, he sat back and pushed the cumbersome thing away.

'If I can't polish my paper, how can I write my poem?' he thought in dismay.

So he picked up his wooden plasterer's hawk instead. The stretched parchment was much lighter than his burnisher and his middle finger fitted comfortably into the handle. He spread sizing on the paper with this tool, to create an absorbent surface for the ink. In more prosperous times, he had used gum arabic, but now he often went hungry himself to feed his paper. The surface of the straw was rapacious, its appetite for rice paste was voracious, but after a few desultory attempts at cleaning the dried flakes off the hawk, he lost heart for sizing too.

'Perhaps I have lost my profession,' he thought, staring at the raw stump of his thumb. 'Or else I have to confine myself to reeds.'

His trimming scissors winked dangerously and the nib knife stabbed at him as he rifled in his pen-case. He chose a reed of middling thickness to convey fear and another that was exquisitely fine, like a thread of black hair, to express desire. But he did not try to carve the pen cusps with his ivory-handled knife. His fourth finger was too weak to command the scissors and the knife too sharp in the angle of his thumb. Instead he pressed the split ends on the wooden cube he kept for that purpose and amputated them like an executioner. A hen, pecking experimentally at the enigmatic reed flakes at his feet, squawked across the courtyard, as if pursued by demons.

A cry of peacocks floated down the hillside and the Scribe glanced up towards the Warden's palace. There were fair women and smooth rag paper behind those gates. The correspondence of the chancery rippled with silver rather than cheap lead; its vellum gleamed with sovereign saffron, vibrant arsenic and virulent copper ore and was as lustrous as the skin of the Warden's Daughter, it was said.

With a faint stirring of desire the Scribe curled his little finger fastidiously to prise open his ink-well in the lacquer pen-case. The heart's calligraphy, as everyone knew, was kohl black, black as the brows of his master's daughter beckoning through the lattice, black as her inky eyes. But the gallnuts he had gathered from the mottled barks of trees beside the river had leaked an unsatisfactory brown stain and been insufficiently wormy for true love that year. The climate here was too cold in the winter, too hot in the summer; the altitude too high and pure for natural bitterness. So he had been obliged to pay for whatever gall he could get and to carry the stain of his disappointments with him. His ink took time to make, but unlike paper this was a solitary occupation. He had his own prescription: lamp soot boiled with gallnuts, strained through muslin, pulverized in the sun and, if he was lucky, turned to paste with coffee and mixed with myrrh before being dried. All he had to do was add a drop of water to the perfumed powder and stir with his little finger.

But at that, his desire was aborted. His well was dry and there was a drought.

He considered his options. There were none. The tools of his craft were ready, and his hand prepared; there was no alternative but to commit a blasphemous deed before the Widow's return. Hesitantly, he rose; uncertainly, he rolled up his mat. With measured pace, he stepped from the shaded archway and laid his writing materials at the threshold of his door. And then with mounting vertigo he stalked across the courtyard. His walking was magnanimous. He sensed himself to be very tall all of a sudden, like a cypress, and lofty in his stride. He stared at his delicate feet protruding under his dirty shift. The recognition was remote and frightening.

As soon as he entered the fusty stable, the goat sounded the alarm and the hens became hysterical. The Scribe wavered in his resolve at the sight of the ladder. And as the treacherous goat continued to bleat, his anxiety mounted. He inched his way up, fumbled blindly in the straw till he touched a warm surface. Then, stumbling down, he swayed back into the transplanted courtyard with his prize, light-headed with guilt.

He hurried into the airless sanctuary of his room, his pulse beating and his lethargy lifted. The egg lay bland in his palm as the squawking hens circled the well, but their necks may have been stretched out due to thirst rather than indignation. Neither the Mullah nor the Sufi's sacks had witnessed the theft. Only the goat could betray him. Breaking the shell in his mixing dish, he extracted the white and stirred his powdered inks into it. As the glossy threads congealed and conjured the coloured dust to life, his pulse thrilled. He might even have enough albumen to bind his pigments instead of his usual substitute of gum Arabic. He could indulge himself!

He prepared his best inks in two small porcelain cups:

the red to represent the continuity of truth; the black to transcribe the fragility of human thoughts. The fibrous albumen gave the ink a gratifying lustre and the luxury of its texture revived his spirits. He was full of energy, invigorated by crime, ready for paper.

But what paper could he use? Where were the luminous sheets of moonshine with the watermark of a star, where were the papers woven with the silk filaments of the sun? Where were the halcyon sheets of beaten gold from Samarkand, the ancient papers spun in the workshops of eastern Turkestan? His nail ached with the memory of them. But these pages were buried in the dust, with the dynasties they had immortalized. An epoch had passed and there was nothing to write on any more but this tickling straw, rolling like dead skin, rubbing like dirt worms under his thumb. 'If I had some of my old master's papers,' he thought, 'I would inscribe my poem in the most excellent style, in the most beauteous script. I would wash it in gold, adorn it with lapis lazuli and rule it in carmine!' But all he had was prostituted straw.

His master's daughter had not looked like a whore. She had approached him like a maiden in a miniature; she had requested a favour like a princess in a poem. She had begged him not to tell her father of it, implored him prettily to keep the secret, and she had asked him in a whisper to write a letter for her on her father's finest paper. It was beyond words beautiful. Would he write to an unnamed lover for her, on the finest paper in the world? He almost swooned at the request; the promised recompense had far outweighed his compromised integrity, although his subsequent remorse, in the visit to a brothel with his fellow scribes, had soon eclipsed these pleasures. But the humiliations of whoring were no worse, in retrospect, than those experienced daily in his profession. He had prostituted himself many times since then.

'Perhaps, since I must start from scratch, I can use some paper that's prepared already,' he concluded, glumly staring at the horny bud of his livid nail.

He searched his piles for a sheet of beaten hemp mixed with humility. It had been formed on a sieve of horsehairs and a few still clung to the chain lines like faint prophecies of pen strokes to come. When he tried to remove them it was like plucking eyebrows. The hemp had not been well combed either, and the fibres had lumped stubbornly beneath the press. The knots tugged at his fingers, despite being burnished, and the pulp had been bleached unevenly in the sun. His eyes wandered across the curious configurations of these sad blemishes. The paper confined him.

He checked the two sides of the page's prison and found them both closed to his face. He paced the narrow precincts, where the ragged edges met at right angles, where the rectangular paper met at the corners. There were no doors or windows in this cell. Once he picked the lock and entered, there were only the chinks between the lines of ink, the gaps between the words, to let him out of this narrow hell.

It was a risky venture. What if he stepped in and found no poem within?

But he was no prisoner; he had no master any more. The page lay blank and waiting. His thumb was sore but his passion was not dead.

But even as he dipped into the winking ink, his poem faded from him. Even as he raised his reed above the page, his dream disappeared. It wavered momentarily, perturbing and eluding him, and then it sank beneath the scummy mould of memory.

He paused. Had the generosity of the poet or the tree summoned him? Did patience or submission give him this right? Had the bridge spanned the river in promise or in warning? Were these questions or answers which he had to write?

He hesitated. And as the last breath of basil pierced his heart, as his dream flooded the reed and the gleam at his nib threatened to drop, he heard sounds and steps approaching. Should he stop or continue? The Widow's shrill voice was drawing nearer, up the sloping hill, towards the entrance of the mosque. She had returned from the bazaar and she was not alone. The strident bleating of the goat mingled with the rough tones of a Kurd and caused the Scribe to press down blindly on the page then, even as ink dropped from his pen. And just at that moment a confounded fly, attracted by the richness of the egg, droned over his paper to investigate the quivering globe of sweetness. His reed stumbled on a snag and splattered to a halt with a compromising blot. The fly settled down to gorge.

His page was ruined.

5 THE REQUEST

I t was noon when the Widow returned to the mosque, triumphant with water and gossip. Her water carrier was a youth with a permanent snivel and her gossip concerned the Warden. But the Scribe was not interested in either and snapped at her rudely when he emerged from his room. When certain quaint courtesies were denied, the old woman was much affronted. She humped off to relieve her parched chickens and offended pride, leaving the Scribe to entertain his guests alone. For her return had coincided with the arrival of a Persian stranger and a Guard from the citadel.

The Scribe shuffled out in his cotton slippers to where the visitors stood awkward and ungreeted under the tattered fig tree.

The Persian had come for the Prisoner's supplies. He was carrying a wizened watermelon, a piece of goat's cheese and some bread scraps scavenged from the market's end. The only other item he was authorized to acquire was paper.

'For the Prisoner,' said the Guard, staring at the Scribe's frayed slippers.

The Persian said nothing.

The Scribe felt a thickening of his blood. His response was barely civil. His paper was not for sale, he said coldly.

The Persian bowed his head, but the Scribe's rebuff did not register with the Guard. He ground his rusty musket into the last remaining herbs unwithered by the summer's heat and repeated his statement loudly, to ratify his own mission, for he was young and uncertain. 'A ream of paper for the Prisoner,' he said.

The Scribe sensed, in the crushing of wild thyme, that this was not a request but a command. The Persian was looking at him through the pungency of herbs with an authority that seemed to have nothing to do with the Warden. It was unnerving. The Scribe felt the ground shifting beneath his gaze. He disliked being ordered to provide paper for prisoners. He resented being compelled to offer what he was unwilling to sell. Criminals should have no right to waste paper, he muttered angrily. If he had any decent paper, he would use it himself.

'Decency depends on need, sir, as gratitude corresponds to relief,' murmured the Persian in response. 'But your hand,' he added, 'proves the worth of any paper.'

The Scribe glowered at the man. He disliked presumptuous strangers, especially those with drawn faces and thin shoulders who tried to ingratiate themselves with elegant puns and courtesies. He supposed the quack had been talking: a miracle denied was a miracle insured, ingratitude proved an undeserved cure. It was doubtless all over town by now. But he disliked hypocritical converse even more than gossip; he had forgotten these arts in his wanderings.

'What about my hand?' he brought out with difficulty.

'Everyone speaks of it, sir,' rejoined the Persian. 'They say you must either have written something of quality in the past or are destined to write wonders in the future.'

The Scribe was startled. He scrutinized the other more closely. And saw the frayed cuffs of the cotton shirt under the cheap *aba*. And recognized a brother in the trade. The man's air of deference and irony betrayed him. So did his ink-stained fingers and his priggish poverty. He was a secretary just like himself, an impecunious copyist!

But should one trust or fear the prospects of such complicity? It was odd. Most sent to this remote outpost recorded deeds in blood, not ink. And most masters he knew were not worth following into exile. This Prisoner, thought the Scribe, must be a master calligrapher, to be accompanied by an amanuensis.

Just then, the water carrier emerged from the kitchen quarters. He shifted from foot to foot beneath the fig tree for some minutes, balancing his two empty urns and waiting for the customary tip. But the Scribe merely bit the dry skin of his thumb and ignored him. The Guard looked vacant. Only the Prisoner's secretary acknowledged his existence with a nod, but the boy had more concrete expectations. When he realized that these were not forthcoming, he left, scoring the dust behind him with vengeful effusions from his nose.

Shame leached into the Scribe's conscience. His initial reluctance to sell paper was complicated by embarrassment. He repeated his disclaimer, but in tones of apology this time. His paper, he muttered, was a poor sort for quality work. It was spongy stuff full of knots and fibres. Despite himself, he was oddly reluctant to offer it to a master calligrapher.

But the Guard had been authorized to permit the exchange of paper, not fatuous civilities. 'The quality is irrelevant,' he concluded, hardening his jaw.

The Scribe expected his counterpart to provide the usual screen of courtesy but the Persian lowered his eyes im-

41

passively. Resistance to another's opinions or insistence on his own seemed less relevant than detachment from both. The Scribe felt his composure fraying before this man who seemed to have mastered the art of the copyist.

'Then I cannot sell it,' said the Scribe abruptly. He was aware of a strange lift in the air, even as he spoke. Since the paper was worth nothing, he would take no money for it, he explained, sensing a stirring on his scalp. Was it the evening breeze or loss of reason? He turned his back on them then, before the Guard could intervene, and stumbled into his room to retrieve a ream. When he emerged from the mosque a few minutes later, he was as stupefied as the Guard was surprised by his behaviour.

The Persian resist to countenance his offer, however, and began to count coins in his ink-stained palm. The Scribe, for his part, would not accept payment and withdrew his hands into his sleeves. The Persian insisted; he continued to resist and the value of the straw paper doubled and might have risen indefinitely in the course of the protracted courtesies, had the Guard not stepped into the breach and pocketed the coins.

'His Honour the Warden will be paid!' he barked. Too late it occurred to him that this act could be interpreted as a bribe; too slowly he saw it might merit a whipping. For a brief second, he hung irresolute between the scribes. But then he thought that perhaps the Warden need never know of it, if the Persian did not tell him. And furthermore, he thought of several ways to ensure the fellow held his tongue. Illogically, his unease was augmented rather than diminished by these strategies, as he ordered his charge to leave. And the deal was terminated in a manner that elicited complex odours on all sides, of crushed herbs and pungent shame.

But the Persian had the last word. As he prepared to follow the Guard down the slope towards the town gates, he turned back to the Scribe.

'I am indebted to you, sir,' he called above the rattle of pebbles disturbed by their departing feet. 'But I promise I shall repay you with paper next time!' At the bottom of the hill, he looked up with his palm pressed against his heart and lifted his fingers briefly to his forehead, in a parting gesture of farewell.

The gesture was at once meek and ironic, but the Scribe turned away furiously and did not respond. Why did the Prisoner's amanuensis think that he might care for them to meet again? Was this a promise or a threat? What did the fellow mean by repayment, if he himself was the provider? Whatever his intentions, the Scribe had no wish for any renewal of acquaintance. The last thing he needed at this moment was the scrutiny of a brother scribe.

He turned his back hurriedly on the two mocking shadows and sought relief in the dim mosque. The visit had so disoriented him that he was under the impression, as he groped his way past the half-opened door of the entrance to the main room, that the Guard and the Persian amanuensis had not left at all, but were still there, mocking him, deriding him, from under the pulpit. And then he remembered that the two humped forms were only sacks.

Could this Prisoner erase the insult of writing on the Charlatan's paper? Some said that life's humiliations could be rendered beautiful by calligraphy. Could he remove the stigma of disappointments, wash away the pigments of despair, draw poetry from straw? He had been told that a true master could purge the heart of hurt and paper of its imperfections. Were such a miracle possible – and it struck the Scribe all of a sudden – then he had lost the finest of reams. Were this Prisoner able to translate tangled fibres into smooth translucence – and it smote him between the eyes like the noonday sun – why then, the paragon of papers had just slipped between his fingers! The one who had come begging had left him the beggar. And with that thought, his legs buckled as he turned away from the torpid courtyard in despair.

He determined to broach the subject of paper with the Mullah that evening. Having lost one ream, he did not wish to waste more. He would ask the old man to delay the dictation of his will a while; he would beg him to wait for new supplies, before writing further codicils.

6 DREAM PAPER

T he weight of the day had lifted by the time the meal was over. The evening breeze dispersed the ebbing heat and smoke from the courtyard, for the Widow had burned her pot and the rice had tasted grey. Although this may have been a continuation of old disasters, she interpreted it as a new one and cast reproachful glances at the Scribe as she sat scraping her charred pot with a metal spoon.

'Another catastrophe!' she wailed. It was an accusation this time. The cause of the Charlatan's curses was freshened by his ablutions and dressed in a clean *aba*. His quilts were aired, his room had been swept clean, and as he sat beside the Mullah on the rug beneath the fig tree, nursing the holiness of his hand, it seemed to the Widow that he was utterly unconcerned by his responsibility for the catastrophes of the world. The burned rice had added to, rather than diminished, his complacence.

'It's another proof!' she cried, with a clang of her spoon. Although her usual refrain was that the charred pot forgives the fire and the burned rice condemns the cook, she felt that both pot and rice could justifiably condemn the Scribe on this occasion.

The Mullah frowned at the sentimental sunset as though it were proof of the Sufi's fate. He was somewhat concerned that his new visitor had not returned from town, for it was late.

But the Scribe smiled as he hazarded his fingers out in the glowing evening light. It seemed very wonderful to have a hand. Any proof worthy of the name depended on paper, after all, he said.

'Or perhaps the words on it,' the Mullah ponderously qualified.

The Widow gave a smouldering scrape to the bottom of her pot.

The Scribe took a deep breath. The moment had come to raise the subject on which his poem depended. Not all paper was worth writing on, he suggested tentatively. Not every page was able to bear the weight of words. Some papers were fine but others blotted too easily. Which was why, he pointed out, pacing his words between the scrapes, which was why, he repeated, gauging each gap in which to speak, which was why it might be necessary to set aside the task of the Mullah's will until such time as the proper paper was available, he concluded in a rush.

The Widow paused, and sighed heavily.

'Proper paper?' quizzed the Mullah.

The straw, the Scribe suggested, could only leave a legacy of blots.

'But when is a blot not a blot?' protested the Mullah.

The Scribe confessed that he had on several occasions been compelled to turn a blot into a word, a word into a blot. Some surfaces were incapable of erasure, he explained, and since meaning was contingent on deletion as well as insertion, everything depended on the quality of the paper.

But the Mullah, sitting in a halo of smoke, was not

interested in crass technicalities. 'Even angels can't delete deeds from the Doomsday books,' he said.

The Widow proved it by spitting into the pot, with emphasis.

The Scribe was nettled into flattery. A man's merits, he urged, deserved better than straw; a person's virtues should be inscribed on the finest paper, surely?

'But errors are written between the lines,' replied the Mullah, with a sad puff.

The old woman contributed a long, cynical scrape of confirmation. The Scribe steeled himself to stretch the metaphor. Straw paper, he tried to explain, made everything look like forgery. It could not sustain failures.

But the old woman had finally heard the fatal word. Even if her failures were evident from the first mouthful, she interrupted hotly, the rice had looked white, even if it tasted grey. And unlike some people, she added, she had not wished to cause offence, for she was a fair cook, though she said so herself. Besides, she quivered, every culinary failure had a cause! At which point, after some furious percussion, she dumped the climactic scrapings on the stone slab beside the well. When the goat nosed near, she ignored it.

The Mullah raised a finger for silence, for the moment was fragile.

'What news from the market?' he inquired, when her spoon permitted.

The Widow had been bubbling with frustration ever since the Scribe had snubbed her that noon. Not even the surface of her news had been skimmed that day.

'How's the drought coming along?' urged the Mullah.

The Scribe felt the conversation slipping from his grasp.

'It's worse than drought!' she blurted finally. 'It's the Warden's couriers!'

Letters had arrived from the Crown Prince with proposals for the Warden's Daughter, she said. And a special envoy was being sent to oversee the dowry negotiations. There was an uproar at the palace.

'His Mother's in a rage!' said the Widow, warming to her theme. 'Mark my words, she'll leave before autumn and the Kurds will raid like they did last year!'

The Warden's Mother was the matriarch of the clan and the liege lady of the tribesmen levied for the defence of the realm. She commanded the Kurds in the hills and her sons in their halls, for she divided her time between them and was wont to lay waste on whoever was not in her good graces. The Warden and his brother were hereditary chiefs of the Eastern and Western Marches but were wholly dependent on their Mother to keep their powers. Since she was a Sunni and adamantly opposed to links of marriage with Shi'ia princes, the mood in the Warden's *anderoun* was naturally everyone's concern.

'Especially as one of the peacocks died of drought today,' continued the Widow, darting accusation at the Scribe. She was beginning to enjoy herself.

The Scribe was prepared to admit to egg theft but did not see why he should be responsible for all the parched birds in town. The Widow, however, had been gossiping with the corpse-washers and had catastrophes of international dimensions to relate. The plague, she informed them cheerfully, had reached Tabriz. The epidemic was an annual affliction, like the advent of a cantankerous relative who came too frequently and stayed too long. And this year's visit had been particularly difficult.

'There's talk of cholera south of the Caspian already,' continued the Widow.

The goat choked and the Scribe swallowed his impatience.

'There's sickness up in the chancery too,' nodded the old woman wickedly.

The Scribe stifled a groan and the goat gagged beside the dry well.

'God's probably punishing the secretaries for spying,' continued the Widow.

But proof of divine intransigence reminded the Mullah that the curfew would soon sound for the closing of the gates and his new visitor might be obliged to stay in the coffeehouse that night. These quarters had been rented by a young Russian recently, who was undermining public confidence and causing a scandal among the pious.

'But perhaps he doesn't have much to lose,' breathed the Mullah, expelling his clouds. 'Perhaps none of us has that much to lose.' It was a cheerless way of arriving at faith, but it gave momentary satisfaction.

The Scribe was about to attempt the cumbersome extrapolation from loss of hope to loss of paper, but though the Mullah had progressed from petitions to wills, he remained impervious to the factor common to both.

'Perhaps I will conclude my will tomorrow,' he said, allowing himself a tentative smile at the sunset. 'If you have enough strength in your hand, Aqa Katib.'

'And enough paper,' murmured the Scribe, making one last effort.

'Perhaps our visitor can take a few dictations for me, if he survives the night,' the Mullah droned on.

It occurred to the Scribe that asking for a reprieve from his duties might be an act of self-erasure.

After a few desultory scrapes, the Widow finally hobbled into the stables, followed by the humiliated goat. The courtyard dimmed.

'It's time to light the lamp,' thought the Scribe, for his

mind was darkening. He did not want to lose the roof over his head.

*　　*　　*

It was the hour of evening prayer and after the Mullah heaved himself towards his duties, the Scribe sat in the gathering twilight, struggling for self-composure. He tried to recall the basil of the morning, but its fragrance was gone. He tried to conjure the poet under the tree, but his dream had receded. It was with difficulty that he struggled to enunciate the credo of his poem. 'It must have no purpose but its own sincerity,' he told himself. 'Its rhythm will be guided by my pulse,' he nodded, without conviction. 'I shall write it with my thumb,' he hesitated. But on what paper?

As he crossed the courtyard, he saw that the door behind the pulpit was still ajar. He lingered to catch the cool air stirring from within, for the mosque walls were thick, the ceiling high, and a little row of windows under the circular dome caught the evening breeze. He longed to press his hot cheeks against the cool plaster. The curfew sounded mournfully. It was unlikely that the Sufi would return that night. But when he stepped inside, he felt as if he had entered uninvited into someone else's home. The familiar room looked alien. He stood stockstill in the unaccustomed obscurity, waiting for the sunlight to set behind his gloried eyes and then glanced around the mosque nervously. There was a growing constriction in his chest.

The dirty reed mats scattered on the floor looked more than usually bereft, and the single yellow ochre carpet seemed more urgently threadbare. Patches in the plaster exposed the crooked calligraphy of tiles around the dome; the walls were pitted as well as daubed, like the skin of bruised pears. Dust motes stirred among the poplar beams and hung down like invisible curtains in the sultry air. For a few seconds, a last gleam pierced one of the tiny window panes and slanted against the ceramic invocations on the wall opposite. The fading shaft, glancing diagonally off the bevelled tiles, tumbled in a pool of pale gold on the lustreless carpet at the Scribe's feet and a sudden lizard raised its flat triangular head from the mottled mat to stare at him with globular eyes of shining jet. He saw an un-bound copy of the Holy Book by the wall; he saw two sacks behind the pulpit steps.

The Scribe stepped closer to peer at the Sufi's belong-ings. One of the large sacks humped on the other side of the pulpit was open. The jute sacking, wrapped in four knotted corners to protect the baggage from the dust of travel, had been untied. The contents were tantalizingly close, con-cealed under a single fold. He hung there, indecisive, irresolute for a moment, and then reached forward to turn back the flap.

The sack was filled with paper. Reams, quires and folios of paper. Pale as pistachio nuts in the crepuscular light, delicate as a breeze in the sultry air. Exquisite!

The Scribe gaped at the reams before him. The paper was subtle, elusive and entirely blank. Each sheet was impeccably trimmed, and as wide as a hand-span of hope. Each page was no longer than belief, and as cool as the human soul. And to his wonder there was something rippling on the other side!

He bent closer and breathed. 'It must be sized with cherry gum!' he muttered. Might the Sufi let him try a piece, just to test the quality? For as he stared, incredulous, he recognized the blooming orchard waiting for him be-yond the silver river. As he stretched towards the paper to lift a piece, he realized that the hand hidden in the green silk sleeve of his dream was about to reveal itself. Now. That very instant. Its appearance was imminent. The poet's hand hidden for centuries was reaching, even as his own was doing, and was going to write a word across the surface of this earth that excelled all other words. It was his poem!

But at that moment he heard a faint sound behind him, a dry cough rustling at the northern entrance. And the stab in his wrist reminded him of his folly. There was a presence at the darkened archway. There was a thin shadow leaning in the dimness, standing with hands folded across his chest, breathing at him. The Sufi!

The Scribe thrust the sheet of paper back into the sack and leaped towards the door. He was suffused with shame. The pious beggar had seen him trying to steal paper! But he had done nothing wrong this time. Nothing except to be caught again, in the act, his heart howled with anguish. A pair of feet on the reed mats accused him of felony. The strangled sound in his throat betrayed him as he ran into the courtyard. For some moments he gagged like the goat by the well and then fled into his room. Barring the door behind him, he sank down and buried his burning face in his knees.

The dream paper! He recognized it even as it slipped between his fingers. He had stolen paper before. He had wooed his master's daughter instead of writing letters. He had been beaten and had run away, embittered. He could never ask the Sufi for his paper now.

For he realized that the Sufi must have travelled across the length of Persia, on foot, just to deliver these reams to the Prisoner. No wonder the Persian secretary had come begging that afternoon; he had expected his own supplies! But how could he have known this paper was waiting for him at the mosque unless there had been some connivance on the part of the Guard? Perhaps he was a go-between for the Sufi and the secretary, and not as obtuse as he had seemed, thought the Scribe bitterly. The fellow had pocketed the coins, after all. Perhaps the Warden had been fooled too, by the Prisoner's paper.

But in the end, it scarcely made any difference whether he had been cheated as a result of magic or mere guile. For what bewildered the Scribe most was why the Persian had accepted his straw at all? Why had he even offered to pay for such rubbish? Was this hypocrisy or some wider magnanimity that extended beyond the confines of receiving? Was this intended as a slight or dictated by a refinement of humility? By what power of detachment had this subtle Persian walked off with his worthless paper, he thought, trembling, and left the Sufi's reams behind?

He cradled his precious wrist and rocked himself back and forth in his misery. He ignored the Widow wailing of pestilence as the night drew in. He barely answered the call of the Mullah who inquired if he were ill. And he did not move as the bats shrieked their white lust against the night. All he knew was the beauty he had lost.

He longed for the Prisoner's paper, like a healing balm; he lusted for it with a burning passion. He hated himself, like a cliché.

RAG PAPER

It was my duty when Layboy to blow a horn and notify
all the men in the mill to come to help press the post.
The man that tended the rag engine was the first one
to come . . . It was screwed down with a short lever as
tight as four men could press and six men pressed the
post till all the water was . . . out. Then commenced
my work as Layboy to separate the sheets of paper
from the felts. To my left hand the lay-stool to place
the paper on; on my right was the post of paper and
felts. The sheets being wet, hardly dry enough to bare
their own weight, so easy to tear, I had to stand half-
bent, all day, to separate them, and when the day's
work was done my back would ache so that many a
night I could not sleep.

Ebenezer Hiram Stedman, 1793

THE SECOND DREAM

At the end of that summer, the Scribe dreamed of a hunt.

He dreamed that he was standing under the pillars of the King's pavilion, in the company of the King's hunters. He dreamed that he was carrying the royal falcon on his arm.

A hood was drawn over the falcon's eyes; its beak was sharp. A spangled turquoise ringed its leg; its traces bound his wrist. The Scribe's leather hunting glove was pierced by its talons and he was aware that his hand existed only for the falcon's holding and his glove betrayed how far he was susceptible to bribery.

The hunters whiled away the hours playing waiting games. Some sat at four-cornered boards of visible chess, lingering over an ivory queen, pondering on an ebony pawn. Others raced their steeds through jasper fields bordered with pearl, chasing polo balls across the quilted clumps of amethyst and lavender. And the Scribe knew from the mallet's crack at the first impress, knew from the clatter of the dice on the board to what degree each man was tempted to transgress. For the King's pavilion existed only to test their playing.

Then the horn sounded and the Scribe knew that the King had come. The hunters shouted that the hunt was on.

The falcon was poised, its head unhooded; its eyes were lovely as topaz, deadly as indifference. And as it lifted off his arm, the Scribe realized that the azure sky existed only for its soaring. The curve of the bird's flight radiating from the pivot of his wrist showed that it was serving more than one master.

But once it had flown, once the King rode on in triumph and his men were gone, the Scribe saw that he had been left there, standing, all alone. He began to chase after the hunters then, and the chessboard existed only for his running. For he had seen a falcon with a topaz eye riding high on the wrist of the last man who passed him by, and read in the swerve and swagger of his gait the signs of overweening ambition.

First he ran through gardens of green malachite, for he thought he glimpsed them, dressed in princely colours, cinnabar red and yellow orpiment, under the dipping orchards at the edge of town. He thought he heard their arrows, piercing the plump quince, shooting the bright plums down. But when he reached the edge of the village they were gone.

Then he looked for them round the bend in the river, through the verdigrised olive groves, where the doe stood in pools of liquid desire, where the mountain goat peered from behind the copper rocks. But he found none of the hunters in the valley.

Finally he ran through clumps of camel thorn, red as lead poisoning, fatally symmetrical. His legs were heavy, weighed down by hackneyed images. The air smelled of sulphur; the sky corroded like sheets of azurite. But he still could not see the hunters anywhere.

Suddenly a stroke of geese rose from a scaling marsh as he ran by. Their wings throbbed, their flight stabbed the lowering sky. And when they fluttered down on the flat chessboard like a flock of loose-leaf paper, the Scribe saw that they had all been pierced through by the hunters' darts. And that was when he knew he was the prey, for the tale of his betrayal had been written in blood-red carmine on those alabaster feathers.

The hunters were at his heels, loud on their horns. They thundered after him, over the stones. And as the falcon lighted upon him, he woke in a panic, with the alarum blowing.

* * *

The horns at the citadel sounded at dawn and at the close of day. They warned travellers that the town was in the grip of cholera. The plague had been chasing at his heels all night and though the Scribe was grateful not to be running still, he knew that he would have to leave the mosque in haste and hurry down the hill.

The fever of the hunt was upon him and the fear. For he was planning to break the quarantine regulations. The autumn caravans had arrived the previous evening but had been stopped at the toll bridge down in the valley. The traders in the caravanserai would be obliged to bypass the town that day, for the Warden had forbidden trade during this season.

But though the dread of his dream was on him, so was the desire. Whatever the cost, he had to find another paper supply. The Mullah's will had absorbed his straw and he had to risk the bastinado for imported rag. He had to defy the Warden's orders and reach the caravanserai before the traders' departure. His poem bit at his heart, hungered at his heels, like a hound.

He lifted the latch to the back door of the mosque,

sniffing the rancid terror of his sweat, and then hesitated. There was a stir at the pulpit door and for a moment he panicked. But there was no further sound among the sleepers. He crept out of the courtyard, leaving the door of his room half open, to avoid noise and invite scorpions. And once outside, he woke with a shock as the freshening breeze whipped against his cotton shirt.

The mountain loomed nearer, bringing a new sound to his ears. From somewhere high among the rocks, delicate as the dawn, feathered like a falcon, a human voice. Perhaps it was the Prisoner in the citadel, chanting.

The wind must have changed, thought the Scribe.

7 EARLY AUTUMN

T he Scribe was preternaturally alert as he made his way down the mountain. He avoided the road and followed the sliding goat paths. He trembled at every thorn bush and cowered at every rock. But once in the valley and under the naked moon, he began to run. Picking his way through the shadowy poplars, he headed for the post house where the couriers awaited the Warden's deliveries. It was at the bend in the river after the bridge, half a farsang north of the caravanserai. He had to accost the traders as far away as possible from the quarantine station, to avoid arrest himself.

*   *   *

When three secretaries succumbed to a virulent disease that summer, no one talked about cholera. Their bodies, blackened by gall and unrecognizable, were thrown into lime pits outside the western walls of the town and life went on as usual.

But the Widow had consulted with the corpse-washers. After days of cramps, the stricken scribes had been reduced to pulp, she reported with relish. They had died shrunk in their sheets, shrivelled to skin and dry as paper, their bowels filled with quantities of enigmatic fluid. In Tabriz, she added, the sewers groaned for weeks with the unpleasant effluence. And when the stages of maceration and desiccation were over and the souls in these human envelopes were fled, a lingering odour was left among the living, which was exactly like the stink of paper-making, she said.

For it was rumoured that paper was the source of the plague. In the past, the northern workshops had produced the finest paper in the realm, but as rags diminished, copyists began to scavenge for corpse cloths to enhance their paper. The deadly disease had thus been spread from page to page, from high court to harem. Gilded decrees and love poems were equally infectious; contracts and leases of merchants and bankers all contained death between their lines. In fact, some claimed that the new edition of the *Book of Kings*, printed recently in Tabriz, was positively dangerous. It was hardly to be wondered, therefore, that by the time the terrible epidemic reached the frontiers of Turkey that summer, the last of the Persian paper-makers had already succumbed to their own craft.

After the unfortunate episode of the burned rice, the Widow kept a wary eye on the Scribe for further signs of biliousness, for the Healer of the People had seen fit to abandon the town during the epidemic. She was much exercised by the news that his talismans now consisted of the Gospels in Nestorian instead of the Quran in Arabic. The Scribe retorted that it probably made no difference to their efficacy as long as the Charlatan was using the same straw paper for both. But the Widow supposed that if paper had caused the plague, then paper must be the best preventative against it.

Nothing else seemed capable of halting the disease. Although the gates were locked and barred across the land, although the movements of travellers and traders were controlled, the paper plague still filtered past unseen at the toll bridges, still floated by the check-points, unobserved. It crossed boundaries like a miasma; it observed no frontiers and left devastation in its wake. Like heresy, the Mullah said. But he would not allow the Widow to wrap her eggs in the Sufi's stock of paper. As long as the Warden refused to grant his visitor permission to deliver his supplies to the Prisoner, it was only logical that the paper too should be kept under lock and key.

For his own part, the Scribe was so afraid of losing his room to the newcomer that he used up his entire stock of straw with savage disregard, in the weeks that followed. Although, he suspected that the Mullah would dictate his will on the Prisoner's paper if he had half a chance, his pride would not let him ask for a single piece. He wished with all his heart that he had never seen those elusive sheets. Indeed, he might even have convinced himself that the phantom paper did not exist in order to avoid thinking of his failure to write his poem.

His spirits rankled all summer and his temper rose and fell with the plague. And since no measures had been taken to stop the disease from spreading, it was hardly to be wondered that the lime pits were soon full. By the time the frontier town between three empires had been stricken for over a month, the Scribe's last straw sheets were finished and he was desperate. Although quarantine forbade all contact with the traders when the autumn caravans passed by from Trebizond, he decided to risk everything to buy a ream of rag.

*   *   *

The Scribe's previous encounters with the Greek trader who sold rag paper had been less felicitous than frustrating. The man always remained mounted to conduct his business, towering centaur-like in Alexandrian dominance among the Turks haggling over peppercorns, the Persians squabbling about paprika, the Kurds bargaining for dried fish beneath the Caspian sun. The last time he had passed through town, he had spread Russian nails, Manchester broadcloth and broken mirrors from Trebizond under his horse's hooves. But the Scribe had eyes only for his reams of rag.

They were smooth and white, the colour of creamed eggs. They were scored with fine grooves which thrilled the fingertips; they promised dimples. The Scribe had wanted to run the tip of his tongue along the edge to test the salt and judge the thickness of the sizing; he wanted to crumble a corner in his hand. For the animal gelatine used on western paper creased in his hand like living flesh.

'Ideal, for an expert like yourself,' rasped the Greek, as he caressed the page.

The Scribe fussed and fingered his coins, but the trader was impatient.

'Three *qerans* for the lot,' he said curtly. It was an exorbitant price. 'You'd only get half as many nails for that,' he added. 'And the broadcloth's twice as much.'

The Scribe was a poor bargainer. He attempted to gain the upper hand by inquiring after mulberry bark but the Greek ordered his lackey to pack up his goods.

'The future's in pulp!' he retorted, and wished the plague on all scribes. Paper sales were of no use unless customers were more gullible or less greedy than this one.

The present circumstances did not promise to improve the Scribe's ability to bargain, but his desperation had enhanced his willingness to compromise. He was ready to pay the Greek whatever he asked this time. These imported sheets were less refined than the wove paper of the workshops, but the risk involved in acquiring them was just the same. My master always cared more for his paper than his daughter, thought the Scribe bitterly.

It was just as well the old workshops had been abandoned, he told himself, hurrying through the poplars towards the post house. Paper in the past had been made with tyranny; it had been wrinkled with misery. If a student grumbled, he would be punished; if he raised the sheets from the mould too slowly, or pressed them too carelessly, or tore the tender pieces hanging on the walls to dry, he was beaten for his laziness. One lad was whipped senseless and fell into the vats and the resulting pulp was grey with undigested pain. The rags they hammered with their paddles were the cast-offs of beggars, the offal of the rag trade, the loose ends of their own misery.

But the reams the Greek brought from abroad were not made with injustice, surely? This creamy vellum was not compounded with sighs. Each sheet was crisply cut and barely needed trimming; each page was polished and required no sizing. Rag paper from the west was beaten by steam-driven hammers, dried on copper cylinders, warmed by coals; it had been polished between rollers, so he had been told.

The dappled moonshine bruised the path treacherously beneath him. The massive mountain lowered like a menacing shell behind. He stumbled, fell, picked himself up again and ran. He prayed the Warden would not arrive before he bought his paper from the Greek trader in the early autumn caravans.

*   *   *

When the caravan came to an abrupt halt at the toll bridge the previous evening, there had been loud expostulations among the travellers. No one was permitted to pass through the gates: neither the traders, nor the couriers, nor even the royal Envoy. Despite the privilege of rank, he too had been obliged to stay in the fetid caravanserai beside the river. He was not pleased with this welcome nor susceptible to the flattery of the Greek from whom he wished to buy some paper.

'Ideal for the expert,' the man had ogled. 'The future's in rag like this!' He claimed kinship with the Georgian by way of the Orthodox Mass, but when he found out he had been cheated of a better sale he called the plague upon all eunuchs.

The Envoy ordered ink and wax to be prepared and pressed the Crown Prince's seal on the sheet grimly. He expected the Khan of the Eastern Marches to lift this petty quarantine promptly, once he saw the eloquence of this blank page. But three hours after sunset, his messenger returned. He had been refused passage at the bridge: the guards were either too provincial to understand the significance of wax or else quarantine, like cholera, recognized no privileges. At that, the Envoy ordered the fellow to be flogged and retired, silently, with a bottle of *arak* and a recently acquired valet. But according to the morning gossip, he may have caught the paper plague himself. When he stumbled out of the caravanserai and fell face down in his vomit by the dry river, the prophecy of the Greek trader was remembered.

The familiar comforts of charcoal were sweetening the air as the valet approached the heaving figure in the brittle moonlight. Did the *jinab* wish for anything, he quavered. The tyranny of a widow's tears had led this boy to serve at court against his will, and he cursed his mother under the left hand of darkness each time his master smiled. For when he chose to break the monotony of his expression, the Georgian's gaze glinted like the cold mosaic on the crust of far-off domes and his smile was as lifeless as a creditor's. The valet recoiled as if stung by a viper at the sight of him, and fled indoors to wash his mouth out with a hot, sweet glass of tea.

The Envoy spat into the dark and drew his soiled robes around him as he turned away from the receding valet. He wished to walk a little along the riverbank before his breakfast in order to compose himself after his dismal dreams. He thought that he was standing in the King's tower, dressing himself in ceremonial robes, when suddenly he saw a maiden spying. She was laughing at him, in the clear unclouded day; she was singing his name out, from on high, and proclaiming to all the court that he was wearing no clothes. He realized in his dream that he would have to climb up the tower to silence her. But when he groped blindly for the steps, he sensed the building falling in ruins about him. And as he woke, he knew that if he stayed inside, the floor would cave beneath him, and if he ran out he would be disgraced.

The eunuch's face grew haggard as he walked towards the bridge. He did not wish to contemplate the embroidered layers of his nakedness. Although his smile had long protected him from public flogging and violent death, he would not retain any expression on his face, if this present mission failed. The ostensible reason for his visit concerned the requisitioning of Kurdish troops, but this public mandate hid a private one. In recent months his smile had proven insufficient to feed the army. When a man's past is forgotten and his present in perpetual negotiation, neither the extravagance of his dress nor the calligraphy of his brows can banish his irrelevance.

He decided to walk as far as the toll bridge along the eastern banks of the river and bribe the guards with the last of his silver. Even if their powers of literacy had been unequal to the task of reading the royal seal, they surely had enough sense to respond to the pressure of metal in their palms. Despite his dyspepsia and the unimaginative valet, his spirits revived as he picked his way along the moonlit bank.

*   *   *

By the time the Scribe reached the bend in the river, it was the maiden's hour, when light and darkness mingled, like milk in the mouth of daybreak. Sunrise and moonfall could be witnessed simultaneously down in the valley but as his feet skimmed the mottled path, the Scribe sensed something else stirring under the double pall of the mountain and the night. Something was moving in the thick darkness on the other side of the river! Quickly, he froze in his tracks, pressing against a poplar, peering between shadow and shade.

Who was there? For a moment he thought he saw a face, pale as damask through the trees; he thought he heard a murmur, sensed a passing whiteness in the air. Was that a maiden, palms uplifted, beckoning like a prayer? But then he came to his senses with the clink of a spur, the jingle of harness, the scrape of a boot on stone. He was not alone. A man was lurking on the other riverbank: a man stood there!

Instantly, he shrank back, his breath slicing a thin wedge between dry lips, his heart tearing its traces. A twig snapped on the other side. The man seemed to be stalking someone, hunting something. Was that a switch in his hand? The Scribe struggled to overcome his fear.

Sunrise wrinkled the hills and the air lightened. And as the shadowy figure turned to mount his horse, it dawned on the Scribe that this was no hunter, no soldier. This was no master of the workshop, ready to lash the soles of a boy's bare feet. The man was carrying a gleaming Turkish sword and not a birch switch. He was tall and distinguished, wearing an astrakhan hat and crimson leather gloves. He was dressed in rich brocade and his wide breeches were gathered at the waist with a topaz buckle.

A chieftain, by the look of him. The Khan of the Eastern Marches! And the Scribe suddenly realized he was staring at the Warden of the citadel. What was His Honour doing out so early in the shadowy orchards?

A cry passed overhead: a summons from east to west.

The Scribe glanced up, distracted. The season was changing, the sun was rising. Was it too late? Had the caravan gone? The Warden must have already come for the couriers! His eyes darkened with dismay and when he turned back towards the other bank, everything looked dim. If the Warden had been there, he was no longer; if a maiden had been smiling through the screen of dimpled leaves at him, it must have been a dream.

The Scribe's mind misgave. He no longer knew whether the hooves were pounding in his heart or round the bend in the river. He was not sure if the clatter and sting of a whiplash were real or imagined. Something was amiss, some unprecedented breach had occurred in his reason.

But perhaps the terror was only as banal and as bewildering as daybreak after all. For the first streaks of sunrise were already spilling over the low hills and pouring across the riverbed like morning milk. Dawn blazed as he gazed towards the bend in the river. For a moment he glimpsed a row of gilded guards, along the incandescent bridge, and then he was blinded. His pulse was racing, his mind dead in its tracks.

Suddenly there was a musket shot down at the toll bridge followed by an answering yelp. The soldiers had arrested someone. So! Some loiterer, some lurker had indeed been hanging around by the river. Cries and scuffles converged, and as the Scribe drew near, he saw a figure being dragged by the soldiers from beneath the arches of the bridge. It was a young man, pale as his starched collar, shouting in Russian, struggling wildly against the guards.

'I'm not a prisoner!' he yelled. 'On my honour. I'm a gentleman!'

The Scribe froze on the opposite banks. He recognized the voice immediately. This was not the person he had seen by the river. It was the foreigner who had begged to buy his straw paper early that summer, the young Russian who had filled the coffeehouse with unclean feathers and impious furs. The soldiers had encircled him with questions he barely understand. He was trying to protect his wire-rimmed spectacles and hardly listening to them. None of them heard footsteps approaching. Nor did the Scribe notice the dim figure drawing nearer on the other side of the river, until the Georgian Envoy stepped on to the bridge and walked towards them all in the brave light of a new day.

Afterwards the Scribe wondered whether the Envoy had spoken, or if it was the sound of his smile cracking that caused the guards to turn. When he drew near with his heavy gait, his arm dangling at his sides, all distinctions between past and present were erased and it seemed to the Scribe that this man was his old master from the workshop, with his pulpy face and hangman's hands.

'Allow me to extend my protection to you, sir,' he began, and his nasal voice traversed the river. 'In the name of the supreme Governor, the Scion of the royal house, His Highness the Crown Prince, whose Envoy I am.'

The soldiers dropped their muskets immediately and fell back, abashed. It was easy, after that, for the Georgian to employ the tarnished silver of his smile and be escorted into town; it was natural, in the circumstances, that he should extend his courtesies to the young Russian, whose naivety appealed to his tastes. But despite his questioning, he could not ascertain from the guards if the Khan of the Eastern Marches was expecting his arrival. All they said was that the caravan had gone earlier than expected. All they knew was that the Warden would deliver his dispatches to the couriers later. More than this they were not authorized to tell.

The premature departure of the caravan was well known to the Georgian Envoy. He had been unpleasantly woken early that morning by farting mules wending their way down the southern road. The regulations governing couriers did not interest him, for he had his own methods to avoid censorship. So he assumed, grimly, that the Warden had instructed the soldiers to keep him out of town.

But the news of the caravan's departure was enough to stain the splendour of the sunrise for the Scribe for ever. If his dream had glimmered before him at the maiden's hour it had completely faded now; his poem had slipped, like paper, between his hands and was gone. He was devastated that his chance to buy rag had been lost. But he also realized he had better slip away fast before he was noticed, before the guards found him under the bridge, before he was reported to the Warden.

He skulked ahead of the Envoy's entourage, breathless as a mountain goat. He scrambled up the slopes, torn by the clumps of camel thorn. A sudden rise of wings in the southern skies left his chest heaving. The summer birds were leaving. And by the time he staggered into the courtyard of the mosque, his feet were bleeding.

The Widow gave him the news. Shortly after sunrise, the Warden had ridden like a fury through the southern gates. No one knew if he had been scouring the riverbank for fugitives from quarantine or had been delivering letters to the dawn couriers, but whichever it was, he was in the worst of rages. He had passed through town, leaving a trail of dust behind him, and had gone straight to the citadel, without pausing for a moment at the palace. Perhaps he was in terror of his Mother, for it was rumoured that a royal entourage was being escorted up the hill that morning, from the caravanserai. Perhaps he wanted to defy her, for he had sent a guard down from the citadel, with a message and a summons. And both were as unpredictable as dreams.

His message was addressed to the Sufi and his summons was for the Scribe. To the Mullah's astonishment, the faith of the former was vindicated, for he had been permitted to deliver supplies to the Prisoner. But to the Widow's consternation, the latter was bound to be punished because he had broken quarantine. She advised him, nonetheless, to change his clothes before being bastinadoed.

8 UP AT THE PALACE

The royal Envoy was conducted up the mountain in grand style, lolling in his litter in the wake of his white ass. He was accompanied by an escort of Kurdish guards, behind a heavy gilt mirror, which was the gift he had brought to the Warden. Everyone thought he had imprisoned the sun. His dazzling prisoner was locked in a gilt cage and strapped to the back of the ass, but despite these limitations, its incandescence opened all gates at a glance and its gleam ensured the eunuch's welcome. No bolts, no bars, no quarantine and no guards could resist his stately solar progress up the mountain road. The capture of the sun marked the end of the cholera epidemic and a change in the weather, for autumn came early that year.

As he proceeded up the slope, the Envoy passed two men along the way. One was an old Sufi struggling beside a laden donkey and the other an itinerant scribe of indeterminate age. When the entourage drew level with them, the Georgian saluted the man with a wooden desk folded under his arm and the pen-case tucked in his belt. He had a certain weakness for scribes.

The Scribe bowed stiffly and quickened his pace behind

the swaying litter. He was anxious to widen the distance between himself and the pious beggar at his heels. He wished to show the world he cherished a higher purpose on this path, for he had not been summoned to the palace for reprimand but for replacement. Since new secretaries had not yet been appointed for the chancery, the Warden needed his immediate services. So the Scribe was going to write on fine rag after all.

But it was not only the stiffening breeze which caused him to thrust his hands inside his sleeves. It was bitter coincidence. The proximity of even finer sheets of paper, fluttering up the slope behind him, whipped at his legs and chased at his heels. Why had the gates opened for him and the Prisoner at the same time? The Khan of the Eastern Marches had absolute command in the citadel and could treat its inmates as he chose. But the Scribe deeply resented the impact of his tyranny on the Prisoner's supplies. He hurried through the gates of the palace as quickly as he could, so he might not see the Sufi, toiling with his precious load towards the citadel beyond.

The town was agog with gossip about the Prisoner that day. All kinds of speculation gathered at the gates and seeped into town like scum. Rumours drifted in the alleys, conjectures floated in the squares, and loose surmise oozed through the baths and the bazaars. And if a thread of fact were caught against the screens of the women's quarters, it merely served, like a watermark, to prove the suppositions.

Some people said that the guards had allowed the Prisoner to wander freely along the riverbanks that morning and had been bastinadoed by the Warden for their negligence. Others protested that the gates were barred all night and that it was not the Prisoner but the royal Envoy whom the Warden saw on his way to the post house that morning. Many of the credulous murmured of miracles, claimed that the Prisoner had been captured by the Envoy after writing himself down to the river at the hour of dawn. A few of the shrewd concluded that he was probably a pawn in the power game between the Khan of the Eastern Marches and the Qajar throne. But the general opinion was that the Warden's fury was aimed at intruders in general, and one Russian foreigner in particular, who was probably more dangerous than any prisoner in the citadel. The hidden hand, they murmured, was everywhere!

But when that hand reached into the reception rooms to hang the Envoy's gift above the door, it was assumed a curse had fallen on the Warden's palace. For who could say his prayers in the blinding face of the sun? The team of swarthy Kurdish soldiers were so distracted by the continuous sight of themselves that had it not been for the Georgian's foresight, the silvered glass would have slipped from their hands on more than one occasion and smashed to pieces on the floor. They were obliged to pockmark the flaking plaster wall with several craters before the eunuch was satisfied that the nail was fixed firmly enough to carry the weight of his gift. When the shimmering ton was finally set in place, it jutted out at an oblique angle over the door, allowing the Warden to see the audience hall behind him at a single glance and the Envoy to watch the Warden's Mother eavesdropping from the women's quarters.

*   *   *

The Mother of the Warden loathed the Georgian's mirror. She also loathed the Georgian, who had filled the palace with the sound of hammers and the odour of stale rosewater all morning. Ever since the Crown Prince had sent his marriage proposals for the Warden's Daughter that summer, she had sworn against any alliance with the Qajar throne, and when she heard of the eunuch's mission, she swore again. But the Envoy's presence posed an impediment to her policy of censorship. With him in the palace, she could no longer control her son's correspondence. If she tried to thwart his activities, she would have to restrict her own. If she kept him out of the *birouni* during her son's dictation, she would have to occupy him in the *anderoun*.

She had stretched her hospitality to the limits that day by spreading carpets in the courtyard and ordering coffee to be served to her unwelcome guest. The cypresses outside the palace walls had been blown askew by the mountain winds, stripped raw to the east and stretching thick branches to the west. But though the crisp autumn breeze was already sending the leaves of the plane trees swirling into the pool, to be nibbled by the rubbery lips of hopeful carp, the air within the walls was still pleasantly mild and bound in by its spicy warmth. Nevertheless, when the eunuch joined her in the smoking pavilion, where her pet peacocks paced sedately to and fro beside the pool, the pale sunshine seemed to chill perceptibly.

In addition to the mirror, the odious eunuch had brought her a copy of the ancient Persian classic recently produced in the new presses of Tabriz. Worse still, he had memorized certain famous passages of the *Book of Kings* in her honour and now lay full length on the carpet, cracking walnuts and reciting, in oracular tones. Neither nuts nor poetry were to her taste and she found the eunuch's posture impertinent. His eyes rolled with the vacancy of his cadences and she wished to heaven he would retire after his morning's exertions and leave her alone. But the poem went on and on.

The Warden's Mother was feeling out of sorts that morning. She had slept badly and dreamed unpleasantly all night. In her dream, she thought she was peering through the grubby latticework of the *anderoun*, trying to see who was below her in her son's reception rooms. Somebody was laughing down there; it was her Granddaughter, stripped of all her clothes! The Warden's Mother had been so scandalized by this unwarranted vision that she ordered an immediate inspection of the kitchens, a thorough beating of the tearoom rugs, and a meticulous search for stray lentils, scattered sequins and tangled embroidery threads in every cranny of the women's quarters. While the eunuch was pitting the plasterwork of the *birouni* for his confounded mirror, she did everything to restrain its irregularities from being multiplied in the *anderoun*.

The *Book of Kings* rustled in the breeze and she tossed a handful of melon seeds with steely accuracy across the pond. Her peacocks gobbled and stabbed among the crackling leaves. The Georgian claimed to be illiterate but she suspected this to be among his various hypocrisies. 'A pox on paper men!' she muttered under her breath.

The Warden's Mother invented curses as a result of boredom, and targeted them, arbitrarily, on whoever offended her. While her antipathies on this occasion were directed at the eunuch, her offence was fixed firmly on her son whom she had sent to the devil on her way to the courtyard that morning. She had told him, in no uncertain terms, that he had better dictate a firm rejection to the Crown Prince's proposals if he wanted to stay in her good graces. A strong-willed woman, she kept her sons in her continuous disapprobation at the cost of their mutual trust. Earlier that summer, because of some imagined sign of disrespect, she had transferred herself, her peacocks, and half the harvest of summer melons from one son to the other, and the Warden did not need to hear his Mother's curses to guess how suddenly she might leave again, if he failed to court her favours.

The old lady had been courted by princes herself in the past and had threatened to kill one too, after submitting to his amorous endearments. They said she still kept the dagger in her girdle. Though years had passed since anyone dared to murmur endearments to her, and the exact location of her girdle was now uncertain, legends of her unveiled daring still echoed in the rocks, still rippled in the mountain streams. It was only when her favourite left her for a Qajar princess that she cast aside her crimson petticoats; it was only when he was shot in border skirmishes that she poisoned her pet falcon and took to her widow's weeds. It was loss of the power to love which made her immobile and of such breathtaking ugliness. But she had retained a residual fondness for her peacocks and her Granddaughter. She had decided that the fat girl's dowry would be worth both the Marches put together, and was determined that a marriage with the Qajars should not thwart these dynastic purposes.

'You have entertained us quite enough this morning, my dear Envoy,' she finally interrupted. For she was bored to death with the *Book of Kings*. She had already flipped through the pages and found that the paper was thin, the ink was smudged, and there were no pictures. The Warden's Mother could not read but she liked looking at pictures. 'It's time for you to rest now after the fatigue of travel,' she said firmly, and she pulled the book from his fat, ringed fingers and abruptly snapped it shut.

'But Khanum,' rippled the eunuch. 'From the moment your son sent his escort for me, Virgo stepped into the house of Venus and all the fatigues of travel faded!'

His smile was hard enough to crack the nuts but so was the force with which the Warden's Mother clapped her hands for coffee to be served.

Her Ladyship pursed her lips on her water-pipe. The eunuch's astrological ironies were tedious, his innuendoes tasteless and his record of events inaccurate. If her son had indeed extended such ill-advised courtesies, she would have known it. But in actual fact, the guards who escorted the odious fellow up the hill had been soundly whipped for accepting bribes at the bridge.

'The way the Khan has trained his guards is a marvel!' he hummed on. 'Such men of Mars! Such heroism in the face of mirrors! I have been royally entertained!'

Besides the Kurds, the rope and the Russian nail, the other source of the eunuch's morning entertainments appeared to be the foreigner whom he had encountered down by the river. The guards had arrested the fellow for spying, but he was only a surveyor, according to the Envoy, desperate for a laissez-passer to leave town. He was much less dangerous than certain scribes he had known, he said.

'All he does is draw maps and chase butterflies,' he added.

'Then the guards were right to shake some sense into him,' said the Warden's Mother stoutly. She gritted her teeth on the hissing mouthpiece and sucked hard.

'They were certainly shaking everything out of his pockets when I arrived,' continued the Envoy, 'but they only found a wax crayon.' The young man had raved about lithography all the way up from the caravanserai, according to the eunuch. He claimed it was the marriage of art and science, the conjunction of east and west, the betrothal of past and future printing methods. And the royal Envoy heartily agreed with him. Wax-writing would outlive the traditional calligraphy, in his opinion, despite the skill of certain scribes that he had known.

The Warden's Mother yawned hugely. She did wish her guest would stop harping on about scribes. Perhaps he had raised the topic of lithographic copies in order to praise their royal original, but she had little interest in His Highness or his new-fangled printing techniques. She wanted the Envoy to take his coffee and retire, so that she could oversee her son's dictation. But though she clapped her hands a second time, the maid was taking for ever to come. And to her disgust, the Envoy had catalogued not only what was in the Russian's pockets but also what was not.

'They didn't even find a scrap of paper on him!' the horrid man was saying.

The Envoy did not add that he had ascertained this fact for himself. Nor did he share his private theories with her about the Russian and his so-called official papers. But he did intend listening to the dictation that morning, and of controlling it too, for her Granddaughter's dowry was worth all the paper in the world. 'Speaking of paper,' he murmured innocently, 'a wandering star tells me that the Warden has found himself a private secretary at this time of general dearth.'

The Mother of the Warden jerked the qalyun closer to the pool and clapped her hands for the maid once more. Scribes again! She could not abide the eunuch. The royal

81

seal dictated his master's will but she guessed that with scribes about him, its shade could extend far. So far, in fact, that when she threw another handful of melon seeds at her peacocks, most of them fell in the pond, causing futile excitement among the carp.

'Paper is such an untrustworthy commodity,' continued the Envoy. 'One never knows where it comes from or where it is going.'

'Our scribes deliver nothing to the couriers without prior approval,' retorted the Mother of the Warden, grimly.

The eunuch wafted his thigh to and fro, but his smile was tight. 'Of course, one can't be too careful with couriers either,' he murmured smoothly.

'The Warden always controls the couriers himself, at the post house,' she answered sharply. For preposterous stories had been circulating about her son that morning. He had been seen prowling through the orchards by the river, apparently, chasing scraps of paper among the autumn mists at dawn.

'Excellent,' murmured the Georgian. 'And who controls the paper supply?'

The Mother of the Warden glared at him. Another sharp clap sent the *qalyun* crashing on to the marble and a shower of hot coals sizzled into the pool. Carp darted about in terror and one of the peacocks fanned a tail at the Warden's Mother.

'Have you worms in your heels, girl?' she hissed, as the maid finally lumbered into the courtyard. 'Where's the coffee? Our guest may leave before we show him proper hospitality!' She wished heartily that he would.

The Georgian Envoy bowed his head. 'I will stay as long as Virgo's ascendance stays the hand of scribes!' he purred. Although she had a sharp nose, with the devil in permanent residence, he had acquired his putrid arts from women like the Warden's Mother. He knew how to force her hand.

'Very good,' replied the Warden's Mother deliberately. 'In that case, we shall keep you here from now on, dear sir. Surely we need not impose our authority over you just to merit your company in the *anderoun*?' And she loosed a stream of smoke through her formidable nose.

The Georgian guessed that this invitation was a calculated gesture of defiance which he could not evade without giving offence. He would far prefer to stay in the auspicious surroundings of these starless heavens, he responded charmingly, instead of attending to tiresome formalities on the earthly plane. This unlettered one, he concluded, glittering with jocularity, would not deprive himself of the rising sign of Venus and the comforts of the *anderoun* for all the world.

'Unless,' he added, lifting a curved finger, 'unless Your Ladyship wishes the new scribe to note my presence for the reasons we just mentioned? I would be loath that any error of transcription on the part of a secretary should undermine your son's reputation.'

A sharp intake of breath stirred the yellowed plane trees and sent a few more leaves spiralling into the pond. Ripples spread wide and smoke funnelled.

'Of course I rest your humble servant,' murmured the Georgian, 'willing to abide by your bidding, entirely at your disposal, ready to follow your dictates.'

He fell discreetly silent as the maid returned with the tray of coffee cups. The girl gave him a wide berth before placing the brass tray at his side. The royal guest was a creature of prodigious manners, and despite his absence of

83

eyebrows, he could imply volumes by the lift of his finger, so they said. When she poured the inky rush of coffee into one of the china cups a few minutes later, the royal Envoy curved a finger into his nostril, stretched his hand across the tray, and flipped the fruitful harvest he had gathered nonchalantly into the other cup. The maid was transfixed.

So was the Mother of the Warden, noted the Georgian. He sensed from the impotence that hovered above the coffee cups that he had scored the first point. He knew from the way she spat thickly into the stagnant pond and stared at the turgid depths that he had won the first round. He had mastered her game.

'Now tell me, Khanum,' he asked, smiling, 'do tell me if your charming Granddaughter is enjoying the gifts I brought her, from His Highness?'

But he did not know that the Warden's Mother had ceased to listen to him at that moment. He did not realize that instead of probing the murky bottom of the pond, she was actually looking at the luminous surface of the waters. She had caught a fleeting reflection of her Granddaughter, peering down from the *anderoun* above their heads. She had seen the girl's serene face mirrored between the pentacle-shaped leaves that floated across the rippleless pool. And she was awestruck, for it seemed to her that the pale oval face reflected between those leaves was unexpectedly beautiful.

She suddenly lost interest in the eunuch. She did not listen to his recitation of her Granddaughter's divine attributes. She did not hear him taking his damned leave of her or see him slopping towards the stairs in his infuriating pink slippers and pretentious Chinese robes. The pimp! She did not even notice his repulsive smile as he took himself off to attend on his confounded honour in the *birouni* below. She was gazing with washed eyes on the surface of the pool where truth was written for all to see, in clear characters, without the need of any scribe.

9 RECTO

T he Georgian concentrated on the attributes of the
Daughter of the Warden as he inched his way down
the narrow staircase from the *anderoun*. She was as heavy as
an ox and as shapeless as a bolster. She had a broad nose, a
low forehead and a perfect forest of facial hairs. And she
was addicted to sugar. When it came to choosing wives, the
Georgian usually favoured fair Circassian women with
pedigrees more limited and faces less endowed. But the
Warden's Daughter would do very well for the Crown
Prince, he thought, as he stepped over the threshold of the
birouni. She would be an asset to the royal *anderoun* and to
himself, he decided, padding across the carpets of the
Warden's reception chamber. For the dowry of this charming provincial could be spread thin to great advantage. And
with that thought, he sat, one knee raised, the other tucked
under his thigh, eyeing his reflection above the door.

The *birouni* was an impressive chamber, two storeys
high, with whitewashed walls that extended to the cob-
webs wafting in the rafters. A frieze of grime in the plaster
coincided with the Georgian's head, and cracks and fissures
fanned out just above it from the row of fretted wooden
screens that opened into the Warden's private apartments.

Better bulk than brains behind a screen, he brooded, peering at the star-shaped holes in the mirror opposite. They were clogged with offended dust and weighed down with years of female frustration. He hoped this affair would conclude quickly, without wasting too much time or paper. If everything went according to plan, he could leave this no-man's-land before the winter.

But a new wife need not stay in favour through all the seasons, he reassured himself, settling more comfortably on the bolsters. As long as she did not bear a son, the Warden's Daughter could be relegated to obsolescence in a few years, being already far gone in obesity. After that, she would soon succumb to melancholy that might resolve in early death. The best marriages, he concluded, glancing at the mirror, were naturally those in which the dowry lasted longer and was larger than the bride.

Although the eunuch had been pleased to note that the gilt frame above the door contained the only mirror, the Khan's reception chamber was festooned with many other trophies. That morning, his host had drawn his attention to the fly-blown British etchings and French girandoles adorned with purple grapes, the plaster cherub from Armenia and the Turkish sword. He took particular pride, too, in a clock from Wittenberg whose ticking, he claimed, would only stop when Divine patience ran out.

Perhaps this was the reason why the Warden was late, and his new scribe had not yet arrived in the *birouni*, thought the Envoy, irritated. An attendant approached, however, with a brass tray to serve him fresh coffee while he waited: courtesy of the Warden's Mother. As the eunuch lifted the cup to his lips, there was a creaking in the balconies above him. A heavy sigh gusted from the dusty apertures and a shower of plaster fell on his shoulders as he looked up to see the Warden's Mother sitting heavily in the angled mirror. The Georgian Envoy hoped the nail was strong enough to carry her reflection.

He frowned, distracted, at the chipped lip of the cup. It was no sinecure to be the head steward of the royal household, responsible for the Prince's escort, as well as chief overseer of His Highness's wives. Despite the inflated titles which the latter received on a weekly basis, these Cradles of Kings and Swans of Sovereignty, these Gazelles of Imperial Glance and Orbs of Royal Corpulence were hard to please and prone to a variety of hysterical diseases. They were also clever, damn them. He pursed his lips as he sipped, for he was fastidious when it came to chipped china.

Since the women were always inventing pregnancies, he had developed a system of divination, based on coffee cups, which combined a reading of the zodiac with interest payments to his personal credit. But cracks in the women's china had recently left him the debtor and the Prince's escort were becoming fractious as a result, for he was in serious arrears for their pay. Unless he could dictate the courtship correspondence to suit himself and keep the dowry of the Warden's Daughter within his sphere of influence, his own borrowings would soon be exposed. His royal master's taste in wives did not concern him. Nor did the machinations of the Warden's Mother. What mattered most was how he could seduce the Scribe.

The Georgian Envoy released a malodorous burp against the back of his liver-spotted hand. The coffee was not sweet enough to his liking and had a musty aftertaste that thickened his tongue. How tedious were the provinces, how flatulent his undigested dreams! And as the Warden entered, followed by his Scribe, he suddenly remembered how notorious, too, was the Warden's Mother, for her poisonings.

*   *   *

The Warden was disappointed by his new secretary's epistolary expertise. He would have preferred to replace the spies sent by the Prime Minister with a less sophisticated local clerk. But this confounded copyist knew all the tricks and betrayed long acquaintance with court protocols. He was never late for his duties, which irritated the Warden exceedingly, and he did his utmost not to waste paper.

There were several reasons why the Khan of the Eastern Marches had to waste paper. The daily contradictions that he faced forced him to prevaricate and so he employed the arts of procrastination and secretarial incompetence to this purpose. Paper dammed up disasters for him and deflected dilemmas; it delayed important decisions and shielded those delusions necessary to sanity. And when the shriek of his Mother's peacocks grew unbearable in the heavy torpor of the afternoons, little balls of paper stuffed in his ears allowed him to catch a quick snooze on the bolsters of the *birouni*, in order to forget the paradoxes that confounded him. He feared his brother would seize control over the Kurdish troops after the Shah's demise, and the only way he could avoid this was to ingratiate himself with the heir apparent. But he also knew that if he did so, his Mother would call on her clansmen and their raids would undermine his authority in all but name. Since he could neither reject nor accept the Prince's proposals for his Daughter's hand, therefore, he needed to give the impression of doing both. But it seemed this new secretary's proficiency and the Envoy's arrival were going to deprive him of this brief reprieve, as well as sleep.

For while his days turned on such questions, all the Warden's nocturnal answers were the same. He was haunted by the Prisoner. He chased him desperately, hunted him restlessly, sought him sleeplessly through the orchards, beyond the goat pastures, down by the river. The wretch evaded guards and gates and dogs, night after night, whatever the weather. One time the Warden followed him half-way to the capital, where he sought an audience with the Shah; another time he scrambled after him to the high passes of Kizil Dagh, causing catastrophic accidents among the winter caravans. Just last night he had stalked his elusive charge all the way down to the post house, only to find him back in his cell at daybreak, locked up in the citadel, scribbling as usual. The Warden was worn out by these waking dreams of his incompetence. Even the new mirror on the wall seemed to be mocking him.

'How gratifying, my dear Warden,' sang the Envoy, 'that your reply to the Crown Prince will be commensurate with the high honour you've received from him.'

The Warden flinched at his reflection. However high the honour, he thought, the Envoy's mirror seemed to have eroded his chin.

'It's difficult to find good calligraphers these days, even at court,' continued the Georgian Envoy. 'There are so many scribblers abroad but few quality scribes.'

The Warden also noted that his face looked crooked in the glass. 'Shall we begin?' he sighed, glancing at the man seated on his heels in front of his escritoire.

The Scribe bowed his head. The sized chancery paper gleamed before him. The ink winked in his pen-case. The stump of his nail had been shaved fine. But his thumb began to tremble as his master came and stood beside him.

'What's this affectation, sir?' said the Warden crossly. 'Why don't you use a reed like the rest of them?'

The Scribe dried his nail hurriedly with the ink rag and rifled in his pen-case.

'But it's his mark of distinction, my dear Warden!' sang the Envoy. 'Ah! The arts of the old school! Why, there was once a scribe, in the court of the Shah –'

'I prefer secretaries with less distinction and more skill,' said the Warden sententiously.

For in his haste to sharpen a reed, the Scribe had sliced his thumb and stained the chancery paper.

The Envoy seized on the new theme. 'I've heard, my dear Warden,' he trilled, 'that the paper officially wasted in the course of a year could stretch from Kurdistan to Khorasan, and from the Gulf up to the Caspian. And as for the unofficial, well!' he smiled and rolled his eyes, 'we all know what the world is made of! They call it the Age of Paper in Europe!'

The Warden was startled to note that one of his eyes looked bigger than the other in the glass. It was true that an unusual flow of paper had been passing through the land. Foreign papers drifted up and down the countryside with impunity. A sneeze on the Turkish borders was now capable of plunging the capital into an ague; an itch on the Russian frontier could lead to scabies in Khorasan. Who cared about assassins when newspapers could undermine the government?

'Women will be wearing it next, instead of veils!' the Georgian was saying. And as the Warden began to stride about, swinging his arm to keep himself awake, the eunuch waxed eloquent on the subject. Paper had replaced all

91

other commodities in Europe, he told the Warden. It was being made into waistcoats and bonnets, aprons and hats; it was being used for curtains and carpets, coaches and litters for the ladies. Bird-cages were made of paper; coffins and churches were constructed entirely of paper. 'Why, even prisoners have regular supplies,' he added chattily. 'Where does it all come from?'

The Warden was afraid he could guess but did not wish to discuss his dreams with a eunuch. And so he did not see the Envoy raising his arched brows at the Scribe, as he yawned.

There were propositions inferred in that look, suggestions hidden in that arch of inquiry, which were not new to the Warden's secretary. He had responded to the lilt of an eye before; he had learned how to read the brows' calligraphy in his apprentice days. And he had also discovered, since then, that there was no need to steal if he were bribed, no reason to beg, either, if paper were offered to him.

But the Khan of the Eastern Marches was unaware of the messages that passed between them. He had just noticed that his nose had swollen as large as his Mother's.

'It's time for the dictation to begin!' he barked.

When he lifted his head, the Scribe no longer fixed his attention on the Warden. He fingered his reed carelessly, brushed his paper scornfully and looked directly across at his new master. The predicted eclipse gleamed in the inkwells of his eyes. Then he wet his lips, pressed his palm down with an arrogant twist, and the pen shrilled across the page. The royal titles blazed with swift, resentful strokes, in carmine and hurt pride.

*　　*　　*

'Scion of the House of the King of Kings, Prince of the Guarded Dominions,' intoned the Warden, swinging his right arm and pacing up and down the room.

The honorifics were endless. They were also ironically inappropriate to the young man they eulogized, who was thin in the shank and rather a wimp, in the opinion of his chief steward. But at least the letter had begun, the dictation had finally started, he told himself. At least the Scribe had proven amenable to suggestion. The only problem was that there might not be any space left for his interpolations.

'Star of Alexandrian splendour and Son of the Shadow of God,' continued the Warden. The inflated syllables echoed among the lizards in the dusty rafters before dissolving in a nasal wail from the tip of the Scribe's pen. 'Viceregent of these Realms and Royal Regent of all others,' he droned.

The Scribe dragged the words across the page and unrolled them like carpets across the floor. He glanced across the room as the Georgian belched in disgust.

The eunuch was suffering from dyspepsia. He had not digested the coffee, and the scratching silences between the bloated titles of the Crown Prince were pockmarked, like the walls around him, with his hiccoughs. He was reclining, eastern fashion, on the Khan's Bokhara carpets, whose glory had been dimmed by the red velvet drapes before the entrance to the *anderoun*. No one ever sat on the two constipated chairs flanking the door opposite that had crawled on spindly legs from the Napoleonic Empire all the way to this defeated end. The eunuch glared balefully at these western furnishings as if they were responsible for his discomfort.

'I offer my life to Your Royal Highness,' continued the Warden. 'May I sacrifice my life,' he qualified. 'Accept my sacrifice, Your Majesty,' he said.

As the eunuch's indigestion and the Warden's grandilo-
quence reached a combined climax with the preliminary
invocations, there was a movement in the winking glass
above the door. The Envoy glimpsed a bulging velvet thigh
against the lattice, a plump brocaded wrist behind the
fretwork, and felt distinctly ill. He realized that he would
be obliged to delete as well as to insert his changes. The
pause was filled by the scraping of the reed and a loud
eructation.

But the Warden had suddenly stopped pacing. 'Where's
your respect, sir?' he said to the Scribe. 'Begin much lower
down and leave enough space to reverence His Highness!'
And with that, he ripped the paper away from under his
secretary's hand.

The Scribe bit his lip and bent his head as the balcony
creaked above them. The Warden, glancing at the mirror at
that moment, saw a shower of egg shells falling on the
domed head behind him, as his Daughter thumped down
in the *anderoun*. But the Khan of the Eastern Marches did
not dwell on the eunuch's discomfiture for long because he
had just noticed the transformation of his own face. It had
been rolled thin and was completely flat under the glass,
like a piece of paper!

WOOD PULP

The American wasps form a very fine paper, like ours;
they extract the fibres of common wood of the countries where they live (and) teach us that paper can be
made from the fibres of plants without the use of rags
and linen . . . If we had woods similar to those used by
the American wasps . . . we could make good paper.
By a further beating and breaking of the fibres and
using the thin paste that comes from them . . . a very
fine paper may be composed, the whitest paper. This
study should not be neglected, for it is, I dare say,
important.

René Antoine Ferchault de Réaumur, 1683–1757

THE THIRD DREAM

One night late that autumn, the Scribe dreamed of a beautiful youth.

He dreamed the youth was reclining on a carpet, with a cushion under his right arm. His languid limbs were robed in silk, the colour of green pistachios, and he was holding a book in his hand, absorbed in reading it. The Scribe was disconcerted by the casual way he smoothed the page with the heel of his palm. He felt obscurely ashamed of the arrogant press of his thumb on the page and was disturbed by the youth's nonchalance towards the book. Had it not been for these defects, the boy would have been flawless.

The Scribe could tell, from his ornaments of coral and pearl, that the hearts of a hundred maidens had been smitten by his loveliness. He could sense, from the lilt of his pavonine plume and the dusky curl which escaped from under his snow-white turban, that this alluring lad was not to be trusted among women. He was the Joseph of great renown, the beloved of all lovers: a myriad poets had written of his fabled beauty.

The marbled book that the youth was reading was a maze of fine calligraphy. But while its right side was made of paper, the left appeared to be a mirror. The right page was luminous and scored with jet-black ink; the left was dim and murky, traced with ink as white as a surprise. And the Scribe noticed, with growing wonder, that while the right-hand page was continually replaced each time the youth turned a new leaf, the serpentine translucence of the left-hand page, where the white ink glimmered, never changed at all.

The Scribe wanted to run forward and pick the sheets off the floor. But they fluttered too far and dissolved in the carpet's flatness. He wanted to lean across the silken shoulder of the lovely youth in order to see what he was reading. But the silence of the book rose off the pages and restrained him like an unborn prayer. To come any closer would be to extend his interests beyond his prerogatives and to intrude on this reader's immaculate integrity. He edged forward, holding his heart; he inched nearer, barely breathing, but even as he hesitated before taking that last step, he realized with a jolt that he himself was being closely observed. There was a maiden gazing up at him from the mirror page!

Beloved of all lovers –! The book was reading him!

He staggered at the sight and almost fell. And as the maiden melted to vapour before his eyes he found himself leaning against emptiness and realized, with a stab of surprise, that the youth was no longer there either. He had vanished too. And the book was gone with him. Only a memory hung in the air. Only the fluttering pages bore witness to the youth who held them and the maiden who had been hidden there. Hundreds of pieces of paper lay trodden to pulp all over the intoler-able carpet, soaking in puddles, rotting in rain. He had to gather them up before they disintegrated; he had to gather them quickly before they dissolved away! And he fell to his knees and scrambled for the sodden sheets as fast as he was able.

*   *   *

He woke with phlegm in his throat, struggling against his clammy quilts. The night had reached the lull point of no return, and the watchman had retired. He could not bear to remember the conjunction of youths and maidens in the damp and disappointment of his bed. As an apprentice he had aspired to harmony between the pen and the page but had since learned that such true marriages are not lightly granted. Although the pages of love are always one, for ever desirable, whoever the beloved; although the paper of despair is always the same too, flimsy and lustreless, whatever the words upon it, the scribal arts had taught him that the human soul is recognized not only by its shimmering in the glass, but by its response to the impress of existence.

According to the manual which he had read in his student days, no scribe had the right to sully a page till he could make it; no copyist could be considered faithful to a text unless he valued the paper on which he wrote it. In the past, it took years of drudge work, months of dreary chores, weeks of scraping the vats and washing the floors before apprentices could use the paper. They had to pound and press and make a perfect page before they deserved to inscribe words upon it. And even then, they only wrote what the master dictated.

But truths remotely glimpsed had now become falsehoods too easily confirmed. Copyists wrote for contradictory masters these days. Paper no longer tested a man's integrity but arrived automatically, with the seasons. It drifted with the autumn clouds around the citadel; it gusted through the homes of tax collectors and sifters of wheat. It flapped through the crumbling caravanserai, out of women's private jewellery boxes and into the saddlebags of respectable merchants. It was stripped from the trees and rolled like scrolls of morning fog across the frontiers, over the rooftops, through the gates of town and across the stubble fields, like auguries of snow. And by the time the ice cracked underfoot inside his chilly shack, the Scribe realized that there could never be harmony between the pen and the page as long as words were interpolated and paper imported. No wonder there were so many fakes and forgeries about these days, he thought, for paper had no meaning any more.

For weeks he had been composing the same letter which was never sent, copying the same letter which was never signed. He no longer knew which version he was writing or to whom it was addressed, but inscribed the pages in a dream. Indeed, it sometimes seemed to him that the recipients of the letters were the same as those who dictated them. He asked no questions; he received no explanations, but the gloss of his privileges at the Warden's palace were beginning to wear thin. And all through the autumn, the courtship correspondence passed back and forth lifelessly, like the facing pages of an unprogressing book.

Small wonder that as the season drew to a close, his own dreams faded. As the days darkened, his poem grew dim. Like mire in the courtyard, mud in the garrison well, it fell in the latrines and winked at him. Like oil turning to sludge, it dissolved in the troughs of the stables nudged by the Warden's horses, nosed by the Envoy's donkey, gathering scum. For his nail had withered to the root and shrivelled to a stump; the passion of his thumb had been dulled and aborted. All he could write on the sheets of chancery paper were trite metaphors and tired images. His poem evaded him.

The Scribe could not go back to sleep beneath his mildewed quilts, for his head was throbbing and his bones ached with the ague. He was sick of elusive youths and watching maidens.

For the worst of it was that all through that autumn, the Warden's Daughter had been staring down at him from the Warden's private quarters. Every time he glanced up from the reception room below, there she was, peeping at him through the star-shaped lattice screens of the dusty balconies. Her wide-eyed innocence unnerved him, caused him to lose all composure. Her avid stare stripped away his newly acquired complacencies. Did she suspect him of complicity? Would she tell her father of his faithlessness? She made him nervous; she made him most uncomfortable. She caused him to squirm and splatter all over the page.

He felt as though she were seeing through his forgeries.

10 VERSO

T he days were darkening and the winds were mean, but the closed balconies in the women's quarters were cosy in the glimmering glow from the oil lamps. Although the Warden's Mother complained of extravagance, the lamps were lit early when the weather turned cold, in order to provide the illusion of warmth. The two screened balconies on each side of the tearoom were girdled round by benches and covered with kilims, and during the chill autumn afternoons, when the western sun blazed fitfully through the diamond panes overlooking the courtyard, the oil lamps created warm circles of crimson and yellow on the Kurdish carpets.

The Warden's Daughter sat placidly in the eastern balcony, cradling her elbows in a circle of saffron light. She squirmed as close as she dared to the dish of sweetmeats, for though she had been instructed in the arts of immobility from an early age, she loved watching her father's secretaries and sucking sweets at the same time.

The hairy-handed Scribe was reading another variation of the courtship letter, his voice as dry as the leaves that had been spiralling down from the plane trees when he first began it. Although they said that the Prisoner in the citadel wrote hundreds of letters in the space of hours, this single letter to the Crown Prince had taken weeks to write and was still not complete. First her father would not let the Scribe begin it on one side of the screen, and now her Grandmother would not let him finish it on the other. But before the letter fell between them, in the empty carp pond of the Envoy's silences, the Warden's Daughter pressed the pages one by one against her heart.

Although she could not see him, she knew the royal Envoy was smoking in the *birouni* below. He had been in a foul temper since the couriers from Tabriz arrived that morning and his water-pipe was still seething. Intermittent gurgles and wafts of smoke were the only hint of his presence, but the sound of his listening made the heart of the Warden's Daughter jump like the carp in the pool when the gardener emptied it in autumn. His silences made her plunge her hand into the dish of marzipan, and sink her teeth into the sticky sweetness. Her Grandmother slapped her wrist.

'Enough!' rasped that presence.

The Warden's Mother was leaning against the fretwork screen and peering down below. Her hair dangled in two oily, saffron-coloured plaits on each side of her jowls; her head was covered by a muslin veil hemmed with tiny sequins. And above her, on a sagging shelf that ran along the length of the balcony, stood cones of purple sugar, rows of Russian tea glasses and a samovar from Odessa that tinkled ominously each time she moved. The twin shelf on the balcony opposite, overlooking the courtyard, contained a collection of Turkish crockery and brass trays from Constantinople. But although the Tsar and the Sultan maintained a balance of power on the balconies, the tea-room between them was dominated by the English Queen, who sat framed in connubial bliss surrounded by rococo roses. The glass of the frame had broken, due to the ill-fated passage of a mule train, and the gilded wood was full of wormholes. But the Warden's Daughter derived wistful comfort from the picture of the royal consort as she nursed her slapped wrist in her sleeve.

The Scribe's voice curled up with the clouds of smoke from the water-pipe below. 'The sweetness of servitude owed to Your Highness emboldens this slave –'

The old lady looked up long enough to eye her Granddaughter's lips made rosy with sucking.

'Far too many sweets!' she hissed sternly.

The Scribe paused in his reading and scratched out a word. 'The servitude owed to Your Highness emboldens this slave,' he read.

'Servitude be damned!' muttered the Warden's Mother, glaring down again.

The old lady was furious with her son. She thought him a craven minion, a paper puppet and a slave of the Qajars. She despised his policy of diplomacy, which did not permit an outright rejection of the marriage offer and was disgusted by his inefficient secretary. For despite the growing coldness of the answers he dictated that autumn, the Crown Prince kept responding with increasing warmth. 'Damn maggots and slaves!' she spat, rocking dangerously. 'One more and I leave!' And she closed her eyes to curse again, for imprecations were the closest that she ever came to prayer.

And her prayers had finally been answered. Much to her satisfaction, when the dispatches were opened that morning, it was discovered that the courier was carrying blank sheets of paper instead of the usual courtship letters from the Crown Prince. An error of delivery, apparently. The eunuch had been furious and had demanded that the fellow be flogged. When the courier protested that he was only doing his duty, the Warden's Mother had intervened, ordered her son to pay the man double his dues and cursed with more than usual freedom all that day. The fretwork screen creaked and the Russian glasses tinkled precariously over her head as she rocked back and forth triumphantly during the reading of the Warden's letter. She was determined that this would be the final draft the Scribe would write. 'Or else, I'm going back and taking the girl with me!' she threatened.

The Warden's Daughter did not mind where she went as long as she could sip tea, eat sweets and hear the scratch of the pen across the page. The *qalyun* resumed its imperturbable bubbling, like a samovar. The Scribe's voice oozed with sugar, his pen rasped with salt just like the pistachio marzipan the royal Envoy had brought her.

He had come laden with gifts. Besides the mirror and the book of poems, he had brought her boxes of sweetmeats: some made of sugared almonds, white as her fingers; others like coils of saffron-coloured hair drenched in rosewater; and a whole tray of tissue-paper pastries, lapped in syrup, layered with nuts. He had promised to give her even stickier ones if she beat him at the little game which he proposed to play just between them. Depending on how many sweets she ate by the time the letter was completed, he would divine the name of her lover in Tabriz, he said. She already knew the name of the husband destined for her on the other side of the mountains, but a lover was something else! They said the Georgian Envoy was clever at divination.

Besides the Turkish sweetmeats, their guest had also brought the Warden's Daughter the prettiest hand-painted mirror she had ever seen. It was made of *papier mâché*, covered with pink and green enamelled flowers, and it had a varnished surface as glossy as the sweets themselves. Her Grandmother had reluctantly permitted her to keep the sweetmeats but had been adamant about refusing the mirror. One in the house was quite enough, in her opinion. So the Warden's Daughter hid it in the bottom of her embroidery box which was made of *papier mâché* too and was covered, just like the mirror, in varnished paintings. When no one was looking at her, she peeped surreptitiously in the oval glass, licking off traces of sugar from her tongue with a pink, cat-like tongue.

'The peace and tranquillity of this slave,' read the Scribe.

The screen resumed its creaking.

'Depends upon Your Imperial Majesty,' he continued cautiously.

As her Grandmother rocked, the Warden's Daughter reached slowly towards the dish of marzipan again. The Envoy's silences pressed against her ears. The Scribe's voice brushed against her heart. She imagined herself eating love-letters, one by one, luxuriously.

'But only such happiness can suffice,' the Scribe read soothingly.

She loved spying on the secretary through the curtains when he knelt before a wooden desk beside her father's door. She liked looking down at him from the *anderoun*, bending over his paper, pressing his reed against the smooth white sheets. Once she glimpsed the black hairs on his narrow wrist, the strange nail scratching suggestively, snuffling the paper, like a living thing. Another time she saw him looking up at her. Her cousins claimed he was Turkmen, because of his salty thumb.

'As shall serve the tranquillity,' he murmured through bubbles from below.

The Warden's Daughter had been raised in terror of Turkmen. Her dreams were thick with them, smouldering with passion, burning with inarticulate desire. Turkmen stalked the women's quarters, their eyes slanted, their breath stirring the curtains. Turkmen hovered in the dust beaten from the rippling carpets, and galloped about the courtyard abducting Kurdish brides. And when she paused near the steps leading down to the *birouni* she could hear the long-nailed fingers of Turkmen scrabbling against the door. She knew that if she ever had the good fortune to be stolen by them, if she was ever strapped on their wild Mongolian steeds and carried off in ecstasy to Merv and Khiva, the imprint of their thumbs would mark her for ever after.

'And the serenity of your sweet sovereignty,' concluded the Scribe.

The marzipan in her mouth dissolved at the thought, and she was reaching for more when her Grandmother slapped her wrist again. It tingled unbearably.

'Enough sweets!' she snapped. 'I told you once already!'

'Grant her a glance of your favour,' the Scribe hurried on.

'Let the teeth of others rot; damn their favours!' muttered Her Ladyship.

'Bestow upon this meanest of creatures,' he continued.

'I won't have him bestowing either!' thundered the old woman abruptly.

For a moment an unnerving laugh rippled up from below but perhaps it was only the gurgles from *qalyun*. The Warden's Mother glanced at her pink-cheeked Granddaughter, with a fat forefinger on her lips. A sweet-faced child, thought the old lady, resuming her meditative rocking. The Hope of the Kurds. Smooth and plump as her dowry, and ripe for the picking with those fine thick brows. Almost beautiful, she thought with a sudden pang, but for the unfortunate rottenness of her front teeth.

'He's already bestowed quite enough,' she repeated doggedly.

The water-pipe paused for another gurgle. The scratching of the reed stopped.

'The Prince's magnanimity is unlimited,' the Warden uttered woodenly.

'His Highness may offer to bestow,' retorted his Mother, with a hiss. 'He may hope to bestow. He may even want to bestow. But I cannot allow –'

'No one,' interrupted the Warden stiffly, 'can presume on his favours.'

'Or his desires,' purred the voice of the Georgian from below. The hand of the Warden's Daughter fell from her mouth. Her Grandmother vented a fulsome oath. Paper crackled, rustled, tore, as the Scribe replaced a sheet.

'If it is Your Highness's pleasure, bestow upon this humble maid-servant,' scratched the Scribe.

There was another gurgle from the pipe below them. The girl trembled and cast down her eyes. She was dizzy with sugar, pink with shame. She attempted to cross her arms around her ineffable girth, hardly breathing. And then, fixing her gaze on the portrait of Connubial Bliss, she succeeded in the effort of self-containment and blinked away the faintness.

'Let it not be said that the love she offers Your Highness –' read the Scribe.

'She's offering nothing!' growled the old woman.

'Is not chaste and has not been tested,' continued the Scribe.

'Taste is better than chaste,' murmured the Georgian in saccharine tones.

The Warden's Daughter stuffed two more pieces of marzipan into her mouth.

'Tasted and found –' repeated the Scribe without missing a beat.

'False!' roared the Mother of the Warden through the holes of the balcony.

There were just three sweetmeats left. The girl gorged on one.

'False are they who say she has not been tested and found true,' the Scribe concluded hurriedly.

Just one more, thought the Warden's Daughter, reaching forward giddily.

'May her life be a sacrifice to Your Highness,' the Scribe rushed on. 'May she be the recipient of your sweet favours –'

Her Grandmother swore under her breath.

The girl groaned. Her head spun as she attempted to stand. But after taking a few steps, the room dimmed and she thumped heavily to the floor. Cries of consternation rose as the oil lamp was extinguished and a broadening stain of darkness spread on the crimson carpets. The Warden's Mother clapped her hands.

'Too many sweets and a waste of oil!' she thundered.

*　　*　　*

The letter reached its inconclusive end that late autumn day and the Warden's Mother noted, with some satisfaction, that there was silence on the subject of further copies.

After his signature was appended and his seal applied, her son did not, as was his wont, inform his secretary that another version might be needed. And before dismissing the Scribe, the Georgian Envoy did not make his usual suggestion either that he should make a copy for the records. They both pointedly ignored the secretary. The Warden found that he had urgent matters to attend to in the garrisons at that moment and the eunuch busied himself decking his white ass with bells in the stables before going down to town. He had been spending his evenings in the coffeehouse, sharing his meals with the Russian surveyor all through the autumn months. It was rumoured that he had been gambling heavily and for astronomical sums.

Whatever the nature of their game, the old lady had taken advantage of his absences to employ the Scribe for her own purposes. She had her private dealings with an Armenian money-lender in the town, who was the sole purveyor of luxury items to this distant outpost and whose interest rates were said to rise according to the amount of paper they covered. She had engaged the Scribe to forge promissory notes in the banker's name throughout the autumn in order to insure a steady increase in the eunuch's debts. But she was disappointed when her son's secretary excused himself hurriedly that afternoon and hastened out of the hall after the dwindling eunuch.

The fact was that the Scribe had nothing left to write on. When he heard the jingle of the Envoy's donkey clopping through the gates, he ignored Her Ladyship's imperious commands to beg for more supplies. For the Georgian's debts had increased the Scribe's dependence on his master; the forged promissory notes had wasted all the chancery paper. He was so absorbed in his own worries that he did not see the Warden's Daughter, etched against the gold and azure windows behind him, gazing after his sloping shadow in the fitful blaze of setting sun.

11 DOWN AT THE
COFFEEHOUSE

The eunuch did not sense the sudden glory on his shoulders when the clouds lifted briefly from the citadel. He was not aware, either, of the shadow loping behind him as his white ass clopped down the hill. He was brooding about paper.

For the letter from the Crown Prince had not gone astray at all that morning. It had indeed arrived with the late autumn caravans, and from its perusal the eunuch was horrified to learn that he had been dead for over a month. According to this pernicious piece of paper, he was already far gone with cholera at the quarantine station that autumn, apparently, and had succumbed to the plague en route to this frontier town. News of his death had just reached His Highness through the traders. The Prince's letter was stuffed with self-condolences. He was griefstruck by this loss, he said. He was heartsick at the untimely demise of his royal Envoy. The plague had deprived the Prince of his trusted servant and the chief steward of the royal harem. The Envoy had been killed off, to all intents and purposes, by paper.

But there was worse to come. The letter had gone on to say that though this death had occurred under the Warden's jurisdiction, the Prince chose not to hold the Khan accountable for the tragedy. Instead, as a sign of His Highness's boundless magnanimity, the marriage proposals to His Honour's Daughter were being instantly withdrawn. The Prince hereby wished to cancel his anticipated betrothal to the young lady, with no prejudice to any of the parties aforementioned, neither in recompense of gifts nor in respect to virginity. He sealed the annulment of the dowry negotiations forthwith, in favour of an increase of troops. And remaining, heretofore, a servant of God and the legitimate son of his sovereign, he signed himself in the flourish of youth, yours in the jaws of hyperbole, the Crown Prince.

The eunuch had naturally taken steps to destroy the letter. All would be lost if the Warden learned of his radical erasure and the cancellation of the marriage suit. And nothing would be gained, either, in remaining alive if the Prince had in the meantime learned how much he had diverted from the royal coffers, or how far his escort were in arrears of pay. Since death was hardly any worse than debt, the Envoy decided to claim the letters were blank that morning. He chewed the wretched sheets of rag to pulp with miserable perseverance and swallowed them down with a glass of sugared coffee, to ensure no trace was left behind. But his burps were particularly acrid as he trotted down towards the coffeehouse in the shadow of his ass's elongated ears.

*   *   *

The coffeehouse was small but it sucked off the sweets of the bazaar like a flea riding the back of a camel. A stream of travellers passed through its doors with the passage of the seasons: rangy camel-drivers with reeking armpits and eyes fixed on summer horizons, pausing en route to Tabriz and Samarkand; wild-haired couriers who thawed briefly into columns of steam beside the roaring oven before walking on across the winter passes of Mah-Ku and through the sleet of Kizil Dagh; spring traders from Bushire who snored over the hubble-bubble under the trickle of the grapevine in the narrow courtyard, with their fat mules waiting patiently under loads of raw cotton and gallnuts for the markets of Erevan. There were always soldiers lingering by the door and citadel guards with their everlasting dice on the steps outside; there were rough Kurds too, who loafed over their coffee cups and laid bets on the length of their virile members, and narrow-hipped Persians who swaggered around the square, offended at the slightest provocation. And then there were the smugglers, the opium dealers and, of course, the spies.

The proprietor of the establishment, a slovenly Turk reputed for his sycophantic ruthlessness, came out to greet the Georgian in the darkened square when he arrived, dispersing the beggars with a stick as the visitor dismounted. The royal Envoy was invariably compared to the Antichrist each time he came to town and was escorted to the doors of the coffeehouse by a wondering crowd, who vied with the white ass for his attention. It was rumoured that the animal's eye was moist with love for her master, but though the Georgian's escort's was equally moist on this occasion, it may have been due to the smells of roast liver and sizzling onions drifting in the rain.

The largesse scattered by the Georgian Envoy was in strict accordance with the expense of entertaining him. His habits were fastidious and his stomach delicate even if his appetites were lewd. His stay in town involved a considerable expense for his host, for he had to be entertained all night and escorted back in a covered litter the following morning. But the Turk's regard was high for his esteemed guest. As a representative of the Sublime Porte, he was careful to maintain the proper courtesies towards the royal Envoy of the Qajars. The smoky cook in the back of the establishment was ordered to prepare a meal for His Honour. A limp youth with a dripping nose was commanded to return the white ass safely to the Warden's stables. And the Turk volunteered his personal services as he welcomed the distinguished Envoy obsequiously into the building. Would His Honour accept the comforts of his private alcove and a glass of *arak*, with the compliments of the house? And of course the young man from St Petersburg would be sent for immediately.

When the young man from St Petersburg had arrived the previous summer, the Turk had taken stock of his weedy neck and tendency to treble and calculated it would take six months to squeeze the fellow dry, if sodomy or cholera did not kill him sooner. The Turk was attuned to spies, if not to the stars. He often said that when the political ground trembled beneath one's feet, the cause was to be looked for in foreign skies. The Russian's starched collars and pretence at science were clear indications that he was on his first assignment. But his host did not wish to provoke an ominous conjunction of the planets. He was wary of the Georgian's rival interest in the youth.

Ever since street mobs had sacked the Russian Legation in the capital some decades earlier, and massacred all but one of its staff, diplomatic relations between the Shah and the Tsar had been severely strained. The new Minister in the capital was quick to register slights and his agents in the provinces were not slow to imagine threats, and from their first encounter at the river, the Georgian too had noted that the surveyor's readiness to defend his country's honour seemed to extend beyond the compass of its lines of latitude and longitude. He assured him that the honour of Mother Russia deserved a study of the almanacs as well as geography and, before parting from him, promised to interpret the stars for the young man. For a certain sum, of course. If the Turk was receiving monthly retainers, in lieu of rent, he was determined to extract some advantage too, from the Russian.

But despite the welcome roubles in the weeks that followed, the Envoy began to wonder whether the long arm of the Tsar or the hand of irony was directing this affair. For it seemed the Russian intended to gain some advantages from him. The couriers, whom he bribed, confirmed that the young man's letters were indeed being sent to the Russian Legation. But although his handwriting betrayed his convoluted purposes, the gaps between his words were disconcerting. The eunuch pretended illiteracy but prided himself on his secret skills of graphology. He deciphered an implicit bargain in these empty spaces. The inference seemed to be that only if he could secure a laissez-passer would the agent consider making any deals with him.

That a secret agent could be double-crossing him was, naturally, not impossible. But when the couriers brought news of his demise that morning, the eunuch had no choice but to submit to the dubious deal. He decided to pretend to provide the Russian with a laissez-passer in exchange for his scribal services; where the Scribe's compact calligraphy had failed to withstand the force of censorship, the Russian's loopy handwriting might possibly succeed. His flourishes offered a wide range of interpretation, after all; the gaps between his words contained the very breath of life. The eunuch hoped that his letters could infer mutiny, suggest rebellion, hint at insurrection in the western provinces. As a result, foreign intervention would be brought to bear on the Warden, and he would be forced into an alliance with the Qajars just to maintain his authority in the region. As long as he did not know the marriage was cancelled, of course. He would submit to the Georgian's dowry terms just to protect his powers. As long as he did not know that he was dead, of course.

It was a gamble the eunuch had to take. Once he played this card, he had no others left. His promissory notes to the Armenian banker had filled the coffeehouse and it was just a matter of time before he would be forced to flee the provinces as well as the court, in order to survive. The season was changing, the leaves were falling. Only the space between the words kept him alive.

*   *   *

The agent thrust eagerly towards the eunuch through the smokers as soon as the latter was ushered into the coffeehouse by his Turkish host. 'My life for yours!' he called too loudly above the crowd. 'I'm glad to see you, sir!'

The eunuch winced but conceded to the listening Kurds.

'How kind of you to come!' gushed the agent. 'As I am a gentleman!' His bombast was limited to Turkish hypocrisy and Persian hyperbole.

The eunuch returned his greetings stiffly. In Russian.

'You know how much I depend on your help!' beamed the other relentlessly.

'We met beneath a lucky star,' replied the eunuch warily.

'And at a propitious moment . . . for a laissez-passer!' persisted the Russian.

Since food had the double advantage of deflecting the attention of the curious and stopping the young man's mouth, the Georgian signalled for prompt service. 'Let banquets be spread in the house of Jupiter!' he called to the Turk impatiently, and installed his guest in the private alcove, brushing aside his inquiries.

'Allow me to serve you, sir, for my own sake,' he murmured, when the fried livers arrived, and then he lowered his voice, for his death weighed heavily upon him. 'I have news for you tonight!' he said.

'Oh sir, you are too kind, too kind!' gabbled the Russian.

The Georgian ignored him. The Khan's horoscope was inauspicious, he confided, very inauspicious. 'I have reason to believe he's suffering from delusions,' he concluded meaningfully.

'Delusions?' repeated his interlocutor through mouthfuls of hot bread.

'He is not subject to wandering planetary influences, sir, if that is what you mean,' continued the Georgian severely. He wanted to strike a serious note. 'These are permanent delusions fixed in the firmament of his earthly mind,' he said.

The Russian bolted down the bread, his eyes fixed on the livers and onions.

'He wants to extend his powers beyond his prerogatives,' said the Georgian, passing him the chipped plate. 'Take this business of taxes, for example.'

The agent took it eagerly.

The Georgian had known some hungry spies in his time, but he had met none whose eating habits were quite so repulsive. 'I refer, of course, to this business of trade tariffs which you experienced at the bridge,' he said, averting his eyes. 'Why, it's a direct provocation, sir!'

'Most provoking,' gulped the Russian. 'The lack of proper papers is most –!'

The Georgian interrupted him. 'But in the Warden's present state, one can ask for no favours, sir,' he sighed. 'He violates international agreements with impunity, as you know to your cost! It's an outrage to your country, your Treaties and your Tsar!'

'An outrage!' repeated the Russian, his moustache working.

'But the Crown Prince is not fooled, I assure you,' continued the eunuch smoothly. 'His Highness has respect for international agreements. If the Warden persists in his delusions of grandeur, the situation will change, sir. It will most certainly change!'

'Will it?' echoed the agent hopefully. 'How?' he asked, his cheeks bulging.

'Don't tell me you don't know, sir!' replied the Georgian with a forced laugh. 'Why, the whole town is talking about it! The mouths of men are full of it!'

The agent drew back his hand from the dish. 'I beg your pardon,' he said, 'I had no idea my laissez-passer was of general interest.'

If there was any irony in his tone, it was deflected by a sudden crash in the courtyard and shouts in the kitchens. Several Kurds rose to investigate the sound.

'Even the stars proclaim it!' said the Georgian, ignoring the interruption. 'One needn't look into the heavens,' he added, rolling his eyes, 'to know that tempests are brewing. All those soldiers pent up without pay, all those guards growing hungry.'

Voices were raised even more loudly in the kitchens.

The storm was growing violent. But the Georgian pressed on.

'He cannot control his troops, sir,' he continued urgently. 'It's just a matter of time before riots occur. The garrisons are grumbling. The men haven't been paid for months! Divine it where you will, the situation's volatile.'

'That's true,' replied the agent blandly, as the wind rattled the doors.

A tremor passed through the Georgian, a doubt without a destination. 'I'm told he's hand in glove with state enemies too!' he added ominously.

There was a roll of thunder overhead and roars from the kitchens.

'Hand in glove?' echoed the other.

Faithful imitation was the first criterion of subterfuge, the Georgian reminded himself. 'The citadel is riddled with heretics and rebels,' he explained patiently. 'If he's conspiring with them and is caught red-handed, that'll be the end of him!'

The agent glanced down at his own greasy hands.

'The situation is more dangerous than you could imagine, my dear sir, its risks greater than you could fear,' the Envoy hurried on, as the rafters creaked overhead.

The agent frowned. Presumably he feared. Or was it possible he imagined? His wire-rimmed spectacles were opaque and words seemed to slip off their glassy surfaces. The Georgian Envoy decided to resort to sensationalism.

'Shall I tell you the worst?' he whispered. 'I depend on your discretion, sir, but I know for a fact that the Khan is planning to marry his daughter to a prisoner!' He fixed the agent with his deadliest smile. 'And the girl's a virgin!' he said, softly.

It was his final bolt. There was a crack in the mountains

above them. And the cook called on God. If that did not grab the fool's attention, then nothing would.

The Russian stared at him. He had paled visibly.

At last, thought the Georgian. 'And if he's ready to marry her to a heretic, what's to stop him from handing his powers to Turkmen?' he rounded. Another blast shook in the mountains and the cook took permanent refuge in religion. 'You see, I've the paper to prove it,' he hissed.

'You have, sir –?' began the Russian, as people scrambled to their feet round him.

'Most certainly!' shouted the Envoy above the growing hubbub, confident now that his words would reach the Russian Minister. 'The Warden is using his daughter to oppose the crown! And the paper to prove it is right here!'

'You have the paper here?' asked the young man breathlessly. He was staring fixedly at the pages which the Georgian Envoy had placed in his lap.

'My dear sir –' began the eunuch, and then took a deep breath. He felt the coffeehouse swaying round him. This was the moment. This was the message that had to reach the Minister. 'You can appeal to greater powers!' he whispered. 'You can turn to higher authorities and call for immediate action. Go straight to the point, sir, and state the facts exactly as they are,' he hissed.

The Russian leaped to his feet. 'My life for yours, sir!' he said. 'But allow me to wash my hands first!'

The eunuch was disconcerted. Was the fellow refusing the deal? He suddenly panicked. Was it too late? Had his death been discovered already? 'My life is in your hands, sir!' he echoed hoarsely.

But the Russian had turned away. Only then did the Georgian realize that the earthquake had caused the ground to tremble beneath him, that rocks were rumbling

on the high slopes, lights flickering along the steep road to
the Warden's residence and horns blowing up at the
citadel. The mosque outside the gates of town was shaking, women were shrieking and men shouting in the
market square. But the eunuch ignored the crush of
cursing Kurds, thrusting their way through the coffeehouse, the Turk who called to His Honour to come
outside, this very moment, for his better safety. He sat
there, dazed, staring in astonishment at the receding
agent, weaving his way to the back of the building. He
gaped in dull surprise as the Russian scrambled up the
ladder to his room even as the landslide thundered down
the mountains. And then he blushed.

*   *   *

The earth tremor loosened rocks that had been unsettled
by continuous autumn rains that night, and sent them
crashing down the mountain on to the Warden's stables.
The landslide swept by the palace and buried the royal
Envoy's white ass beneath a pile of rubble, but it spared the
town. Everyone said it was a miracle.

But as far as the Georgian was concerned, it was a
catastrophe. He realized that not only were his debts
unpaid, his mission aborted and his humiliation certain;
not only was he dead to all intents and purposes, but a fool.
He had assumed he could do what he willed with a scribe.
But he had underestimated the impenetrability of pure
innocence. And with that admission, an old forgotten rush
of blood rendered him as naked as a rose. His ruins fell
upon him then, and he attained the distinction of feeling
ashamed.

He rested on his elbow and stared for a long time at the
sheets of paper scattered pell-mell round him all over the

floor. The Russian's incorruptibility and his own folly were written there, across these mirrored surfaces, in plain characters for everyone to see. If he could turn these pages and cast this scribbled copybook of life behind him, if he could countenance the great erasure lying ahead, his death might prove to be the miracle after all. But whether he would have the courage to face the blank pages lying beyond his reach was quite another story.

He was so deeply engrossed in contemplating the paper that he did not see the Scribe at that moment, stumbling from the dark courtyard at the back, groping blindly through the dim coffeehouse, towards the pitch-black door of the night beyond.

12 LATE AUTUMN

W hen the earthquake shook the town, the Scribe lost his balance on the ladder and tumbled headlong into the stables behind the coffeehouse. He crawled across the sodden courtyard on his hands and knees. He passed the opium smokers who took no notice of him and the Georgian Envoy whom he barely recognized, and he finally swayed out to the crowds in the market square. He did not know what he was doing until he found himself passing through the southern gates of town, and only realized his destination when he stood before the Mullah at the mosque.

*   *   *

As soon as he had heard the tinkle of the ass's bells turning at the gates, the Scribe decided to follow the Envoy down to town. He crept out of the darkened courtyard and picked his way through the bituminous puddles and slippery streams all the way down the slope. For the late autumn caravans had brought no replenishments for the chancery that morning and he was desperate for paper. Besides, the smooth surface of his master's ironies had become cracked of late, his sarcasm had grown more brittle; his remarks had begun to compromise the listener as well as the speaker and the Scribe was growing jealous of the time he spent in the company of the surveyor. He suspected paper was slipping between his fingers into Russian hands.

For there was a paper crisis in the country and very little was being imported by the traders from the West. Paper was at a premium and demand had quite outstripped supplies. Rags were being used up more quickly than people could be impoverished, so they said, and such was the zeal of occidental street collectors that bundles of bones were sometimes accidentally carted off along with the rags to be stamped and pounded to paper. Whether due to heartlessness or efficiency, this state of affairs could not continue. According to the newspapers, all the western paper mills would either have to come to a complete standstill, causing huge financial losses, or else beggars on both sides of the Atlantic would have to be reclothed. Since shareholders did not wish to suffer the economic consequences of either eventually, rags had to be transported over long distances. Certain manufactories had even resorted to shipping mummies from Egypt. Yards of corpse cloths from the pyramids, strips of stained embroideries unwrapped from bulls and ibises, cats and princesses were being tossed into the paper vats over the seas. And this coarse brown paper was being used in groceries, bakeries and butcher shops all along the eastern seaboard, so they said.

Small wonder that a paper hunt was underway across the world. Since manufactories were chewing cotton rags and spitting them out in seconds, churning linen scraps and drying them in minutes, pressing them flat and polishing them in a matter of hours, there were insufficient raw materials to keep pace with these furious machines. And so awards were being granted to whoever found a substitute for rag. Gold medals were being given to anyone who could make vellum without linen; silver medals were being offered for wrapping paper which did not depend on cotton. Some people had tried beetroot and others, wasps' nests. One scientist had experimented with eighty varieties of vegetables. Others had used broom and swamp moss, marshmallow and water wool, jute, grass and lime-tree bark. And a year ago, it was announced that a man in Saxony had succeeded in making paper out of trees. English journals, currently printed on small regulation sheets, would soon be published on wood pulp, and the Russians were in hot pursuit of the patent.

What kind of paper could be made from living trees, pondered the Scribe. Was this dream rooted in reality? Could such paper be harvested each autumn and revive each spring? It was bound to be a rare commodity in Persia, he thought, for where could such paper grow in these barren lands? Unless, of course, the country had been turned to a paper desert already by Mongol hoards and raiding Turkmen in the past. Unless the very trees of paradise had sacrificed themselves so that the books of creation and revelation might be inscribed on these never-ending scrolls. Perhaps the Sufi had travelled from the south on a magic carpet made of paper, mused the Scribe. Perhaps the Georgian Envoy was gambling his life away for this priceless commodity each evening. As autumn drew to a close, he became obsessed by the idea that the Russian had somehow acquired the precious pulp.

His desires ran ahead of him as he descended into the darkness of the valley. He followed the glimmer of the white ass through the narrow alleys and entered the main square of the town behind it, unobserved. A few cobblers and tinkers were still plying their trade under the arcades of the bazaar, warming their knuckles in the light of little braziers, as the Scribe slipped past. But he did not linger for the Georgian to amble by the glaucous fountain. He did not wait for the rag-tag beggar boys to gather hungrily round his ass. He had already slunk behind the beggar at the door, concealed himself inside the coffeehouse, hidden himself among the opium smokers. And when he saw the surveyor thrusting his way effusively through the crowd, he sloped silently through the smoke towards the courtyard at the back. By the time chicken livers and fried garlic were being served in the private alcove, the Scribe had crept into the stables and was climbing up the ladder to the storeroom. For he was determined to ransack the room for the foreigner's illicit stock of wood pulp paper.

*　　*　　*

The pestiferous lodging in which the student from St Petersburg had installed himself the previous summer was hardly more than a winter store for animal fodder. A hole in the floor at the back of the room dropped into the stables, and steps in the front led down into the coffeehouse itself. The only furniture was a wooden couch across which a cotton quilt had been hastily tossed and the only window a small aperture cut into the sloping roof, stuffed with fistfuls of old straw, which the laconic Turk removed when he first showed it to his lodger. The quilt betrayed evidence of earlier indiscretions and the wall bore the stains of previous heads. And as he scattered the straw on the floor, the Turk kicked a scrap of paper out of sight and tried to rub the smudged grime off the pitted wall with his palm. A futile gesture.

'This place is as filthy as the caravanserai!' said the Russian as he came up the steps. The schoolboys who had watched his every move since his arrival pressed after him curiously. The light was dim even in summer and the air stale. He peered at the tell-tale marks along the wall and assumed they were ants. Or bed bugs.

The Turk's shrug might have been interpreted as deference or indifference. He remarked, pointedly, that Englishmen had been quite satisfied by his hospitality.

When he asked if additional furnishings were required, the Russian had looked around the room hopelessly. A blackened oil lamp indicated all that might be expected from the establishment, but further comforts seemed remote. The uneven floor hardly deserved the stained rag of a carpet and the outhouse was perilously close. The Russian was disappointed, for the trim Armenian he had met in Tiflis had promised him better lodgings when he heard he needed banking services in this outpost. The jeweller's wife, however, had objected to having a foreigner in the house, for fear it might provoke her neighbours. He was stuck here until he could acquire official papers authorizing his departure from the town.

He told his landlord, in stilted Turkish, that his room would serve him well enough. And he added that although he did not smoke, he did expect to write and needed a supply of paper. On his producing a handful of roubles, an escritoire was miraculously produced, and one of the urchins swaggered off, in giddy privilege, to purchase a ream of cheap straw paper from the local scribe. But it was only later, when he was alone, that the Russian allowed himself to scrutinize the row of smudges on the wall.

They proved to be digits, numerals on the march, odd and even numbers scribbled on the grimy plaster. At first, he supposed they were measurements of altitude in these mountains; then he assumed they were calculations of spherical trigonometry related to the tributaries of the river Aras. Afterwards he wondered whether they might not reflect observation points in the night skies. But they proved in the end to be dates, including that of his arrival and his long-anticipated departure, dates of the comings of couriers and of the goings of caravans. The contemplation of these digits concentrated his mind wonderfully as he waited for his laissez-passer with a retinue of schoolboys trailing behind him through town.

The Russian, as he plainly stated to anyone who cared to question him, was a cartographer who had lost all his scientific instruments together with his pack animals and a flock of sheep over the high passes on his way to these borders. His sextants, his compasses, and over a thousand pieces of blotting paper, intended for drying specimens, had tumbled into the abyss en route to this town. He had seen his theodolite with horizontal and vertical scales winking at the bottom of a gorge; he had watched his metal tripod smash a hundred feet below. All the broken lenses of his telescopes, dazzlingly near but irreducibly far, had twinkled at him down among the rocks. He had also lost several crates of Russian sugar, his grandmother's excellent brandy, and some supplies of cherry jam to drink with tea. It had been a catastrophe.

But nothing was more so, frankly, than to find himself in this backwater in the first place. Due to a fatal detour and the perfidy of an Englishman he met en route, he had believed himself closer to Bokhara than Baku. The Briton had given him a detailed map from Astrakhan to Astrabad, and had recommended a false route which sent him among Turks instead of Turkmen. Although the direction had looked credible enough on paper, the rivers and mountains he followed led from nowhere east to nowhere west all the way to the wrong side of the Caspian! He was determined to leave as soon as he acquired the proper papers to do so, of course, and while waiting for permission to depart, he recorded all that he had done since he arrived. He kept records of his findings for the Imperial Russian Geographical Society, scribbling maps and calculations on every scrap that he could find. So it was hardly surprising that the Scribe believed paper to be the foreigner's main concern.

*   *   *

The Scribe climbed the rickety ladder to the room above the coffeehouse with a mounting sense of vertigo. As he emerged at the top, he paused to catch his breath and calm the beating of his heart. It took some time for his eyes to grow accustomed to the cramped darkness, for the only light in this low room, filtering in fine threads from the coffeehouse below, was full of the fumes of undigested opium.

After a few moments, he groped into the alien terrain feeling like a thief. He found his bearings by the creaks in the floor; he calculated his position by the rustles underfoot. The wind wheezed through the straw in the skylight and thunder rolled overhead as he crept cautiously into the uncharted dark. But the room was thick with dreams that were familiar to him. He half fancied the velvet eyes of a doe glimmering before him, the flutter of a goose feather above, the touch of a hyacinth at his hand. He smelled the odours of crushed basil leaves and thyme beneath his feet, and, finally, the stink of rotten pistachios, which he traced to a sack of mildewed nuts by the steps leading down to the coffeehouse. It was only as he felt for the oil lamp and touched the fluff of dream dust on the floor that he recoiled in horror.

Once he had light, he began his quest in earnest. The surveyor's specimens were stacked in the back of the room, near the hole above the stables; his writing desk lay on his couch, where he might take advantage of the small aperture in the roof. And along the walls extended an undulating range of maps that threatened avalanches at every step. There were papers everywhere: under the carpet, beside the bed, below the skylight, and the Scribe hunted through them all.

He began with the straw, which he had himself sold to the foreigner the previous summer. It had been used as a substitute for blotting paper for all the specimens whose implications had so scandalized the Mullah: the tell-tale death of leaves and maidenhair fern, the murder of seed pods and camel thorn. He deciphered the faint signatures of sacrificed butterflies and the bitter tale of beetles on the spongy surfaces. He read the voiceless woe of broken-winged birds and shrivelled lizards, the dry despair of plants scrawled across the pages around the trapdoor entrance.

Then he searched through the sheets of rag paper which the surveyor had acquired from the Georgian Envoy through the autumn. They were covered in maps of unknown lands: multi-coloured empires spreading across endless furlongs of kermes red and copper green, mysterious countries of turmeric yellow and cobalt blue, magic islands of porphyry and jasper. There were mountains of paper, hills and misted valleys of paper, narrow gorges and distant passes, deserts and seas of paper that beckoned him over the frontiers of the familiar to the borders of the unknown.

But there was not a single sheet of wood pulp among them.

Finally, in desperation, he opened the escritoire and scattered its contents on the rumpled quilt. Surely he would find new paper here, some sheets of the precious patent? He groped among dirty collars, rifled through shirt studs, caught his nail on a cuff link and stabbed himself on a silver falcon pin. But his hunt was fruitless. Though he found a bone button scribbled with talismans of the Charlatan, he did not feel the living forests of paper rising like sap between his fingers. These notes scribbled with digits could never revive next spring. These crumbled scraps covered with arabesques and looping letters were certainly not rooted in reality. There was nothing here which could bear the imprint of his poem.

It seemed to the Scribe at that moment that all the trees of hope were felled in his despair. The wind sawed in his ears and the hail rattled overhead. The beloved of all lovers had abandoned him and the world stretched blank and paperless before him.

It was just as he was about to give up and creep back down the ladder that he saw something glimmering on the floor, hidden beneath the straw. As the tempest roared and rocks rattled down the mountainside, a piece of paper flickered in the storm light and lay like a summons between his feet. One sheet! It winked like an eye. It gleamed like a mirror. It beckoned.

And even as he bent to pick it up, he realized it must be a piece of the new paper, the true paper, the revolutionary paper made from Russian trees. Here it was, one page of the unbounded forest on which to write his dreams! But there must be more where it came from. Where was the rest, he thought feverishly. He must have missed the place where the Russian kept his secret stock –

But before he could turn to look for any more, there was

a terrible cracking in the high passes. A shudder shook the
mountain and roared down the slopes. At that moment, he
heard a creak, he saw a shadow rising on the stair, and
someone loomed behind him. He had been caught in the
fatal act of theft once more. All he had time for was to draw
his narrow head beneath his hood and step back blindly. All
he had breath for was a gasp, as he dropped the paper and
fell into the abyss of loss. When the surveyor stumbled
against his oil lamp on the steps from the coffeehouse, the
Scribe had already pitched headlong through the trapdoor
to the stables below.

But even as he fell, he saw the white writing on the
mirror page. He had wasted paper and betrayed his scribal
arts; he had lusted for paper more than he had ever loved in
his life. His worst fears were confirmed: he knew then that
he would never be a poet. And with that thought, he fell
headlong through the lost years, with his dreams shattered
to pieces around him.

*   *   *

Much to the satisfaction of the Warden's Mother, the
mirror of the Georgian Envoy crashed to the ground and
broke into a thousand pieces during the landslide. But the
earthquake caused no further harm within the Warden's
walls, although it shook them. The women of the *anderoun*
ran shrieking into the open courtyard in the middle of the
night, but they only suffered from lost dignity and nobody
died.

Besides the Georgian's white ass, the only other death
that occurred was that of the limp youth who had accompanied the pampered animal back up to the palace. A
water carrier in the summer seasons and a stable hand at
the coffeehouse the rest of the time, the youth had not

achieved great renown in the town. But despite this and the permanent drip in his nose, he still harboured the distinction of human dignity and hidden hurts, he still remembered disappointments suffered during the drought. But he found little of remunerative value under the mattress or in the writing desk of the Scribe, when he chose at the very moment of the earthquake to nose about his room. When the roar of rocks swept through his disenchantment, burying him alive, no one knew of his indiscretions, however, and so he died with his honour intact. His mother was wont to claim that her son had been sacrificed to a higher cause, and remembered him for years, with maternal tenderness, in conjunction with the Envoy's ass.

The broken mirror may have been construed as an ill omen and the loss of the ass involved some recompense, but the Warden's Mother was content that both hastened the departure of their guest. For the royal Envoy returned to Tabriz soon after the earthquake, wending his way through the stubbled cornfields in the wake of the winter caravans. The only legacy he left behind him was a heap of promissory notes in the coffeehouse, which proved most profitable when stuffed into the Russian's meagre quilts. Although he never obtained a laissez-passer for the Russian, one man's debts did help the other survive the winter. But despite the fact that these proved great enough to undermine the mountain, the monumental laugh which shook that matriarchal edifice at his departure caused more tremors than any earthquake. Gone like a fart, she said, and good riddance to him.

Paper also saved the Widow's life that season, but although they felt responsible for her later death, the Mullah and the Scribe never guessed the role they played in this earlier survival. When the landslide swept down the mountain, bypassing the town by inches, it shook the ceramics off the dome of the mosque and scattered the names of God all over the threadbare carpets. The blasphemous shock of this reprieve was so great that the old cleric had been uncertain whether it was premonitory of future failures or the consequence of previous sins, but as soon as he saw the Scribe standing outside his door that night, he sensed that the alternative between these was more unnerving than either possibility. For he had to admit to his former secretary that the Sufi had occupied his rooms since autumn, and was obliged to turn him away. The docility with which the Scribe accepted this news was utterly unpremeditated. His acquiescence filled the old man with such remorse that he swore to forgive all faults from that time on, including his own heresies. Since winter threatened and the Widow was inclined to rheumatism, he dismantled the tottering towers of paper accumulated in his room that very night and relinquished half the drafts of his will to her, so that she might line her boots with them and tuck them under her petticoats against the chill. Thus although the Mullah was not wholly reconciled to dying intestate by the scope of pity, and the Scribe remained still unaware of the high distinctions merited by humility, the Widow owed her life to both of them on this occasion, and to their unconscious acquisition of those attributes best served and most valued when merited by the nameless and the traceless of this world.

SILK PAPER

Legend has it that Emperor Wu tried to procure a suitable paper for the printing of money and to this end consulted with the wise men of his realm for advice. One of the learned suggested that counterfeiting could only be prevented by mixing the macerated hearts of great literary men with the mulberry pulp. The Emperor is said to have taken the suggestion under advisement, but at length he decided it would be a grave mistake to destroy the literary men of China simply for the purpose of using their hearts as ingredients for paper. In talking over the problem, the Empress suggested that the same result could be achieved without interfering with the lives of their scholarly subjects. The wise Empress brought forth the thought that the heart of any true literary man was actually in his writings . . .

Summary from Ch'ûan-pu t'ung-chih,
1833, recorded in *The History of Printing
of Early Buddhist Sûtras*, Tokyo, 1923

THE FOURTH DREAM

As the winter snows fell, the Scribe found himself dreaming of a maiden in a tower.

Everyone was agitated by the maiden in his dream. Princes and ministers conferred about threats to the state; grooms and squires whispered of insurrection. And an old beggar woman wailed and mourned and cried catastrophe at the gates. For the maiden had been discovered unveiled in the court, singing without consent. No one knew how she had entered the King's tower so brazenly or who she was to dare to sing in his absence. High under a bright blue dome of turquoise tiles she chanted, her voice as clear as the unclouded day, and the birds in her heart provoked a marquetry of agitation.

The Scribe recognized the maiden immediately. She had a promised voice, crisp and green as heraldry, forever new and threatening as spring. He knew he was supposed to deny that he had heard it. He could not admit that this song was familiar to him, if he wanted to keep his head on his shoulders. For the maiden's voice was as shameless as gules of blood on damask, as vernal as a sudden thaw. It revealed the naked truth to all the world.

The courtiers were divided in their opinion about this

flagrant exposure, this invasion of composure. They paced their steeds and marched about the irreducibly flat fields discussing the maiden's identity, disputing her lineage and making perspicuous observations about her chastity. Some wrote impromptu defamations of her virtue with the greatest possible decorum; others walked around the tower measuring the thickness of the walls, the depth of the moat, debating how the maiden had laid siege to it. They could not understand why their calculations melted at her song. They could not decide if she should be relegated to the stables or promoted to the royal harem where she might control the King's other wives.

Despite her dangerous impertinence, the Scribe knew the maiden was innocent. Although her song threatened, he was willing to sacrifice everything to possess its purity. He was ready to risk his neck to reach her. But though it was day outside the turquoise dome, it was night within and he had to climb through moonlessness towards her. The worst was that he would have to pass the beggar woman at the gates.

The old hag was blind but canny. She was like an orthographical error in a derivative script. As he stepped into the tower, he felt her near him, sloppy in rope slippers, stained with smears. He felt her groping up the uneven stairs after him, breathless with blots, panting with lack of space. The higher he climbed, the more remote became the maiden's voice and the closer at his heels hissed proof of his poor penmanship. Finally, even as the pure sound faded altogether, the beggar woman grabbed his legs and he felt the tower disintegrate about him.

Its arches broke over his head, its walls gave way, its overlapping tiles, green and black as melon rinds, split open in mid-thought and fractured beneath his feet. Traceries of flowers cracked in cynical ceramics around him; crude bricks protruded, frescoes flaked on each side. Finally, the plaster shattered under the interrupted roof and the tower fell in ruins round him.

And when the Scribe saw the frosty stars mocking him through the broken beams, he finally realized there was no maiden there at all. He had been fooled. There were only the owls hooting at him in the ruined tower and the old beggar woman crying shame upon him. They were denouncing him to the princes, telling all the world he was a forger and a thief. And as they scoffed and jeered and derided him, he understood his dilemma with terrible clarity. If he ran out from the collapsing tower, he would be humiliated; if he stayed inside one moment longer, the buckling floor would cave under his feet and engulf him.

*　　*　　*

Icy screams woke him. He was bewildered by the wails for the corpse-washers and the summons for the exorcist. The turquoise stars seemed to be echoing the piercing cries. He wondered if someone in the palace might have died.

The Scribe shivered. Since he had almost lost his head with his belongings during the earthquake, he had been allocated chancery rooms by the Warden when the heavy snows started falling. But although these lofty chambers had quartered scores of scribes in as many seasons, he was the sole secretary employed up at the palace that winter. The shrill of his predecessors' reeds and the curls of their chill breath across the page were most discouraging. He slept between their cold quilts and wrote with their congealed ink. He suffered frostbite in their footsteps and finally acquired a fine wool *aba* and a tall lambskin hat to deflect their ghosts. But when he woke from his dream that morning, nothing could protect him against their quivering condemnations. The souls of the dead were reminding him that a true scribe should be his own master.

The Scribe had given up self-mastery that winter and his sense of failure had deepened with the snow drifts. For the wood-pulp paper that finally began to flow across the Russian borders had proven to be a dreadful disappointment. Each page was uniformly smooth; each sheet was trimmed as neatly as a coffin. But there was no bark or twig to graft his words on, no leaf or root of hope among these reams. The pages were whitened by acids and emptied of meaning; all life was bleached out of them. He could barely trace the pulse beneath the screaming saw or feel the sacrifice among these faceless pages. The Mullah's will had rustled with more promise on the summer fig tree. The autumn correspondence crackled more convincingly in his hands. But this long-anticipated wood pulp passed like fog before his eyes.

Small wonder, therefore, that despite its superficial whiteness the Russian paper seemed to grow sullied with the Warden's demands that winter. For new chancery secretaries were expected from the capital, and the Warden needed a spy to watch the spies who would be sent to watch him. Throughout the darkening months, the Scribe had been obliged to use his craft for suspect purposes. He told himself that no copyist was perfect, no calligrapher unerring. He argued that errors were an occupational hazard in his profession. He tried to persuade himself that faithfulness could only be distinguished from forgery if one could read and write between the lines. But he wished with all his heart that he could wipe the tablet clean. And in the absence of further inspiration, he gazed with shielded eyes on dazzling upland slopes, in search of the perfect page of snow.

The dawn he dreamed of the maiden, the Scribe began to think that perhaps he himself had died. Certainly his dreams were dead. They had all been scattered, cast aside and separated since he had submitted to the dictates of others. Only the fat girl, he realized, had not imposed her will on him. Like his master's daughter who had asked for his own heart's desire, she never made any demands. She had been peering down and watching him through the screen of the women's quarters all this time, without dictating a single word to him. As he lay shivering in the blue-black darkness, with the cries of distress and consternation echoing in his ears, he felt her modesty, as soft as vellum against his cheek, inviting him to his calling. His dreams of being a poet were dead but perhaps he might write a manual for scribes instead.

13 WINTER

Many were killed by the cold that year or suffocated in the attempt to keep warm. The winter was the worst in living memory. Tears froze on people's cheeks and ink turned to ice on the page; water congealed in the bowels of mules and in the beaks of peacocks, and two dogs died of barking the night the Scribe dreamed of the maiden. Everyone assumed the Hope of the Kurds was done for, too. She lay bleached and bloated in her choking room with the brazier burning blue under the warming quilts and the air poisonous. Her eyes had rolled up beneath their lids, they said, but when the paper was pulled away from the door jambs, the gulping girl came to her senses and leaped to her feet with staggering agility, her breasts heaving under embroideries of snow.

The Warden's Daughter may not have wished to be resurrected in the presence of her cousins because she burst into tears on regaining consciousness. Her Grandmother was so upset to hear her bleating like a goat that she summoned the Charlatan immediately. Although he had taken refuge with the Presbyterians during the plague, the quack had resumed his activities in town at the onset of winter, with denunciations of the old world and prognostications of the new. He was hailed as a prophet when he returned and was welcomed back with open arms, not only by the women of the marketplace but also by the ladies of the Warden's residence. His popularity reached such heights that, to the Scribe's dismay, he even acquired a permanent footing in the garrisons. Indeed, had it not been for the scepticism of the Warden's Mother, he would have insinuated himself even closer, for while the Scribe performed his duties in the *birouni*, the Charlatan attended on the daily ailments of the *anderoun*.

Although she had resisted his palliatives all winter, the Warden's Mother succumbed to the quack that morning. Even the most cynical of natures abhors a vacuum and when doubts stretch too far, faith is sometimes the only rational alternative. Her preoccupations with her Granddaughter had far-reaching political consequence. And besides, there was a matter of some intimacy, a delicate personal female subject which she needed to broach with the Charlatan.

For the matriarch cherished a dream which depended on the Hope of the Kurds. She had been planning for the girl's marriage since her birth: the dynasty would be saved by her, she thought, the future inscribed on her, for the gap between her teeth had always promised sons. Everything depended on a certain auspicious event which had been anticipated all autumn. But despite close observation and a calculated diet of bullock cream and mutton tails, despite exacerbated jealousies and strained tempers in the *anderoun*, this long-anticipated change in her condition had not yet occurred. The fat girl's menses had not begun. Given the shock of this morning's waking, moreover, and the current temperatures, the Warden's Mother feared that it never would. She wanted the Charlatan's assurance that the blood had not frozen in her Granddaughter's veins.

The palace was frigid that day. The night had been so cold that several of the coloured glass panes in the balcony of the *anderoun* had snapped and fallen out of their diamond frames at the first touch of the sun, scattering rainbow particles all over the floor. Splinters of sapling green, wine red, and limpid yellow ice melted on the carpets and the uncompromising chill of absolute light filled the tearoom. Every scrap of paper in the palace had to be used to stuff the broken window panes against the white dawn wind.

The Healer of the People arrived from the garrisons, red-cheeked and steaming, and ordered the Hope of the Kurds to fast on dried rhubarb and worm seeds from Bokhara. He also prescribed a paper compress and recommended dream interpretation, every morning, as a diuretic. The Nestorian Bible would serve, he averred, for it was religiously and scientifically permeable, both the paper and the printing having been produced by machines. It was a miracle that the young lady had survived the excessive superfluity of her dreams, he added portentously.

The Mother of the Warden saw, at a single glance, that the Nestorian Bible would not serve. The ink smeared off the page and the size of each sheet barely covered her Granddaughter's bosom.

The Charlatan was feeling expansive in his new and privileged role and the Scribe, distorting records for the Warden in the *birouni* below, was distracted by the familiar tones drifting from the screens. He squinted up suspiciously.

'One must find ways,' boomed the inspired Charlatan,

'to void imagination's bladder of superfluities accumulated at night.'

'I have my ways,' said the Warden's Mother darkly. The balcony creaked.

'But does Your Ladyship have enough paper?' asked the irrepressible Charlatan.

How had the confounded quack wormed his way into the presence of the Warden's Mother? thought the Scribe. He tossed aside the flimsy sheet on which he was scribbling.

'In Europe,' continued the Charlatan grandly, 'paper proves the value of a thing.

The Scribe gritted his teeth and started a new page. The tea glasses were tinkling precariously as Her Ladyship rocked back and forth above.

'Look at those virgins in their veils!' continued the quack, with a calculating glance at the sugar loaves. 'I swear, paper could enhance a girl's value a hundredfold!'

The Warden's Mother frowned at the purple cones above her head. Whatever the resemblance between them and her sweet-faced Granddaughter, she was not sure she wished it to be increased a hundredfold. But perhaps paper might keep the girl warm.

'In Europe,' repeated the Charlatan, 'everything is wrapped in paper!'

It might incubate her, thought her Grandmother. Like a blanket round yoghurt.

'It guarantees quality and improves the sales,' trumpeted the quack.

It might absorb stains, thought the Warden's Mother hopefully.

'Consider watermarks,' trumpeted the Charlatan.

The Scribe's hand jerked. He had botched his record.

Watermarks in paper were invaluable against forgery, the quack was saying. The crime had proliferated so much that threads of silk were being woven through banknotes now, to ensure their value. Invisible lines and mystic signs were rolled into the pulp to verify its worth. Forgery was the sin of the age, he boomed, and watermarks the antidote.

The Scribe's features darkened in the *birouni* below. He began to collect his pens together and prepared himself to leave. He could not concentrate on his counterfeiting.

One of the American printers had abandoned the Presbyterian Mission because of watermarks, the Charlatan continued relentlessly; the man had undergone a crisis of faith due to the number of forgeries he had committed without being detected. Why, he himself had seen a small, black watermark on an envelope which had travelled all the way from Philadelphia to the Salt Lake without depending on a single courier.

The Warden's Mother stopped rocking in her astonishment. Had hidden symbols been pressed between the Crown Prince's correspondence? she wondered. Were secret signs also concealed in the pernicious *Book of Kings*? She was sure that pictures had passed before her eyes when the poetry was read aloud on winter afternoons; she could swear she had seen lions and unicorns, deer and dragons embedded in the paper. It was bad enough that dispatches continued to flutter over the mountains thick and fast all winter, but that this correspondence could be independent of couriers and replete with invisible messages was appalling. For despite her bribes, the Crown Prince's courtship had not abated after the Envoy's departure. Or so it seemed to the Warden's Mother. And His Highness's tone did not suggest that of a rejected suitor, either. Quite the contrary.

He sounded as if he had scandalous expectations of a dowry, from what she heard.

'Now I could sell Your Ladyship some straw paper,' the Charlatan was saying hopefully, 'that could provoke puberty as well as safeguard virginity, all at once.'

The old woman was gratified that he had deciphered her deep concerns. It was a relief to know that he could read between the lines and understood her worries, without her having to put them into words.

An exorcism of evil influences was essential, he insisted. But if the household was to be properly purged, all remnants of catastrophe should be thrown out first. All splinters of coloured glass from the broken windows, all fragments of cracked mirrors caused by the earthquake, all spurious imitations, fraudulent reflections and false reproductions, including the Scribe, he trumpeted, should be relegated to the goats. The Warden's secretary should be sent packing, because – and at this he lowered his voice to whisper the awful truth – the fellow was a forger. And having diagnosed the greatest threat to her Granddaughter's originality, he smeared the walls with daubs of red ochre paint, and charged according to the drips. The paint ran down a little way before freezing against the plaster, like a pale gold cage around the shivering girl.

But when he tucked the sugar loaves under his arm in payment and took his leave, the quack discovered the Scribe waiting in the *birouni* below. The Warden's secretary did not defend himself against the accusations but just stood mute beside the door as the Charlatan shuffled past. His silence was uncharacteristically acquiescent.

*   *   *

149

The Warden's Daughter was not sure she wanted to tell her Grandmother what she had been dreaming that morning. For the truth of the matter was that while she had been lying comatose beneath the poisonous quilts, she had dreamed of the hairy-handed Scribe. She dreamed he was dressed in silken robes, the colour of green pistachios, and was writing in a book. Each time his hand turned the pages, her heart flipped in her bosom; each time his pen touched the paper she knew he was writing her lover's name. But as she drew near to see what it was, something impeded her. A heavy bolster, a stupid cherry-coloured velvet pillow was slipping from her arms. She had been so worried about dropping the wretched thing that she almost fell and thrust her hand out to stop herself. And then the Scribe vanished. She had woken exhaling her face into the frozen air, with her cousins screaming around her.

The Warden's Daughter avoided words. She submitted with bovine acquiescence to the teasing of her peers and the punishment of her elders for she found it was a double loss of truth to speak. As a result the women did not pay much attention to her. Though she was nagged, she was not often noticed; though she was teased, she was largely ignored. In fact she could imagine situations because of silence and the tyranny of oversight.

The imagined self of the Warden's Daughter floated about, diaphanous, in the women's quarters. Unseen by her aunts, with hairs sprouting in their nostrils, unknown to her cousins, with pinching fingers, and quite invisible to her father's various wives, whose stomachs were full of wind, she drifted over the walls and through the windows in the most delightful situations. No one knew about her wanderings, least of all her Grandmother. Light as a silk scarf, she danced about the palace, unconfined; slender as a peacock's feather, she floated in and out of the male and female quarters. And she looked exactly like the varnished maiden on the lid of her embroidery box.

The situations depicted on the girl's embroidery box were flat but full of meaning. The cherry petals bloomed precisely where they should; the cypress tree contained the perfect quantity of birds. And the varnished maiden, pressing her lips with her fingertip under the flowering cherry, was just like her imagined self glimpsed in the oval mirror hidden in the box. There was a youth, too, who plucked languorously on his lute nearby, and the Warden's Daughter saw that despite their being separated by a silver stream, the two figures shared an undivided destiny. Their almond eyes slid sideways towards each other; it was obvious that they were fated for each other. How heavily the carp plopped in the stream between them! How tellingly the maiden glanced towards the youth! She recognized him immediately, of course, for his thumb proved him to be the Scribe.

The Warden's Daughter always imagined situations with the Scribe. It was easier to clean grubby lentils and mildewed rice when she could think of him; it was possible to squeeze wet cloths and peel the slithery skin of beetroot because of him. She imagined him plucking at her heart as she sewed seams in sleazy velvets during the dreary afternoons; she imagined his gaze resting on her as she sorted the stupid sequins in heavy trays in the *anderoun*. And if the cruelty of cousins, or the ravage of aunts, or her Grandmother's questions proved unbearable, the Scribe would always save her. All she had to do was to imagine a situation and he would lift her up and sweep her diaphanous self away on the steed of his thumb. The women in the *anderoun* were only aware of the disappointed envelope that was left behind.

After the Charlatan left that morning, the Warden's Daughter was propped against the wall of the *anderoun* under the portrait of Connubial Bliss, and her envelope was filled with the foul infusion every half-hour. Since the relentless regimen had been maintained since dawn, a desperate if humble urge had been building up within the girl. She swallowed the worm seeds uncomplainingly in the hope of being ignored but no one would leave her alone. She was surrounded by terrible attentions.

The aunts plied her with the purgative as they poked at their pieces of embroidery. The wives commented on her bloated appearance as they made deft music on the large brass tray of white rice, piling little stones on one side, heaping clean grains on the other, and sweeping avalanches down the central slopes. Several sisters-in-law suggested enemas and thought sewing might help her keep her mind occupied. Her cousins tickled her feet as they tried to chafe them and offered to wrap her hands in sugar paper to keep them warm. And although the eruption of younger children into the *anderoun* afforded momentary distraction, the only way their mothers could hush them was to draw their attention to the Warden's Daughter, squirming in the middle of the carpets.

'Watch the big girl being fed like a baby!' they cried. Shamed by the awed stares of the little ones, the Warden's Daughter kept swallowing until she was ready to die. The worm seed stung her throat, her bladder sang and she began to shiver uncontrollably. She sat on the floor like a muslin bag of dripped curds, with her embroidery box clutched tightly on her lap. If only they would let her alone! The varnished maiden was swaying perilously beneath the cherry tree; the youth was plucking urgently under the cypress; and the river swelled ever wider between them.

Her Grandmother scrutinized her whey-faced Granddaughter. The exorcism seemed to be working. She was beginning to rock back and forth, like a brooding pigeon.

'Perhaps it is infectious,' said an aunt nervously.

'Perhaps she's pregnant,' whispered one of the wives wickedly.

But when they forced the cup of worm seed to her lips again, the fat girl began to blubber for the second time that day. The matriarch leaned forward to listen to her sobs with keen interest. She noted her little moans with growing satisfaction. And when she finally saw a dark pool spreading on the carpet where her Granddaughter was sitting, she knew the dynasty was saved, the Eastern and Western Marches would be united, and her sons could be controlled at last, under one absolute and condign rule. Her own!

'Perhaps she's starting her courses at last!' pronounced the Warden's Mother triumphantly, and ordered everyone to quit the room.

But when she saw her Granddaughter was dripping like a spent fountain in the middle of the sopping carpet, when she realized that the poor child was innocent of all maturity except that acquired by humiliation, the Warden's Mother felt a dangerous melting in her bosom. And with her heart bursting, for pity's sake, she swung round with a violent oath towards the tearoom door.

The women had hardly the time to scatter out of the way before she opened it on their faces. She wished the Scribe to be summoned to the *birouni*, she thundered, and her son to prepare for her descent, without delay.

14 A COLD DAY

A messenger toiled back up the snowy slope from the town later that morning in the company of a large white umbrella. The arrival of a sunshade in the middle of a snowstorm caused a stir in the women's quarters and conjectures were rife about why the services of a jeweller were required at such a time as this.

But the Warden's Mother had summoned the Armenian to the palace because he owed her a favour. The owner of the only umbrella in town traded sugar for lapis lazuli and bartered Russian glassware for arsenic, but she had also seen to it that his banking services had become commeasurable with immortality. Ever since the Georgian's ignominious departure, the banker's interest rates were said to be as high as heaven, his debts as deep as hell, and his promissory notes of infinite duration, and so she expected a good bargain from him in exchange. In addition to his other merchandise, he sold large rolls of paper, in bulk. Although the old lady was illiterate in the ways of ink, she was well versed in sweat and blood. She knew the Charlatan's wrinkled straw was incapable of absorbing her Granddaughter's dreams. She also guessed the restricted chancery rag was inappropriate for the limitless Hope of the Kurds. And so she sent a message asking the banker to bring his entire stock of industrial paper up to the palace immediately and summoned the Scribe into her presence at the same time, to keep a strict inventory of her purchases.

When the Armenian received the message, he responded promptly, despite the foul weather and the funereal expectations of his wife. Although he had lived on the wrong side of frontiers all his life, he was an optimist at heart, bridging his conversations with maxims he did not understand from languages he had not mastered. He liked to state his prices at strategic moments, when his customers were distracted.

It seemed a strategic moment. The day was unpropitious and the mood in the town savage in the aftermath of a long winter. A fatal accident had occurred in the coffeehouse and piles of paper, abandoned there since autumn, had caught on fire and gone up in smoke the previous night. The Turk was roaring for revenge and the jeweller's wife, a lachrymose woman, was full of trepidation. She had dreamed that her husband had been taken up to the citadel by the Warden who had ordered his mouth to be stuffed with unpaid promissory notes. So she implored him not to go.

But the Armenian was a man who liked to oblige, especially where profit was concerned. Who could say, he temporized, whether her dream was a prophecy or fulfilment? For he had already suffered from one financial disaster that autumn. His sugar had tumbled down the mountain, his mirrors had been smashed at the bottom of the deep gorge, and paper was all he had to show for it. Lengths of wallpaper, painted with peacocks, extracted from smugglers along the Turco-Persian border; rolls of lace paper, embossed with birds of paradise, requisitioned as recompense from the Greek traders in the clearing houses of Tabriz; and most unexpectedly, sheets of miraculous cellophane ordered by mistake for missionaries to print their bibles, in Nestorian. No one had ever seen such quantities of paper. Vast barrels, massive drums and gargantuan vats had been employed to produce these rolls of ever-lasting width and length. Manufactories that stretched from east to west had been filled with the fathomless, flocculant pulp; cylinders of immense dimensions had moulded and pressed it, rolled and dried it. But in the last analysis, who needed so much wallpaper or perforated *papier linge*? How could he sell transparent cellophane from the New World without attracting the suspicion of his creditors in the Old? So when the Warden's Mother said she wished for a confidential sale, he thought the cherubim had interceded on his behalf.

His wife sobbed that he was making her a widow for the sake of paper, and begged him not to oblige. But her husband assured her that he would be protected. Some months before, an impoverished debtor from Philadelphia had offered him an umbrella in exchange for a cancellation of interest, expressing the hope that it might shelter its bearer under the protective shade of Christ's Mission Abroad. And although he kept his interest rates unchanged, the Armenian had accepted the gift because it promised to cover him from all contingencies – above, below, before, behind, in heaven and on earth. 'And especially what lies between them,' he added confidently, as he left his blubbering wife. On reaching the palace and shedding his bundled shawls in the Warden's antechambers, therefore, he insisted on keeping his umbrella with him, and was ushered into the *birouni* holding this singular article over his head.

*　　*　　*

The first thing the Warden's Daughter saw, when she peeped down through the balcony screen, was the Armenian's white umbrella advancing across the carpets of her father's reception rooms. The second was the Warden's secretary, seated by the door opposite. His chin was high, his eyes bent low. It was an enigmatic pose, which caused her some excitement, for he had placed himself far away from the epic matriarch across the room and as near as possible to her.

She was experiencing a brief reprieve after her morning miseries. When the Warden's Mother had descended like an avalanche down the narrow steps to conduct the paper negotiations in the *birouni* below, the regimen of worm seed was relaxed and her prying aunts and cousins were locked outside the tearoom door. Cocooned in solitude, the girl revived. She piled the entire day's fuel on to the brazier, and began to relish her situation. She imagined herself whispering through the screen at the Scribe. She imagined him glancing up to notice her. And she stuffed herself with jellied petal conserves and pink quince jam on fresh bread, brought hot and papery from the ovens.

The Scribe proved less ardent in reality, however. Although her spirits rose at the sight of him, she was disappointed at the focus of his attentions. He ignored the Khan of the Western Marches pacing back and forth, remained oblivious to her Grandmother, and responded to the white umbrella with awe-inspiring neutrality. Instead of seeing her, he stared fixedly at the sheepskin under the jeweller's arm.

'God preserve Your Ladyship!' offered the latter, in his breeziest bargaining style. 'Heaven preserve us from whatever lies between! Everybody's talking of it!'

The Warden's Daughter drew back as her father rolled his eyes wearily. Although the Khan of the Eastern Marches had resolved one cause of sleeplessness at the end of autumn, his nights had been worn white since the start of winter by another. For after submitting to his Mother's will over the courtship affair, he had been obliged to acquiesce to the Crown Prince's demands for extra troops. If rumours of these concessions spread, he would forfeit his Mother's favours instantly.

'Why does everyone have to talk so much?' he mumbled.

His Daughter could tell, from her father's voice, that he had been pacing to and fro again, all through the night. She dreaded meeting him in a situation, fast asleep. After a few moments she found the courage to look down once more.

'About your Daughter and the coffeehouse,' the Armenian was saying. He had decided that news of the fire would distract attention when he named his price.

The girl drew back again as her father frowned. She wished she could be the subject of a situation rather than a conversation.

'What's my Daughter's connection with the coffeehouse?' growled the Warden. The girl imagined herself, briefly, in the coffeehouse and quickly abandoned the idea. From what she had heard, the place was as public as the tearoom of the *anderoun*. She preferred more private situations. Her Grandmother was poking the depths of a nostril with a square of muslin and appeared not to have heard the question, though you could never be sure with her. The Warden's Daughter noted sadly that the Scribe was preoccupied too, with the contents of his escritoire. So she turned her own attention to the bottom of her jam jar.

The Armenian settled his sheepskin strategically between his dreadful client and the door. He was telling her father that the coffeehouse was a hotbed of perversity.

'And "a Turk's wrath is more than other men's"', as they say!' he sang. Had the jeweller said 'Turkmen'? The Warden's Daughter glanced down again cautiously and saw the Scribe caressing the page. She closed her eyes and shivered –

But her father's pacing had disturbed her Grandmother. 'Well? Where's this paper, then?' barked the old lady, flaring her nostrils for fraud. Idle talk annoyed her, particularly when she could not hear it. She preferred numbers to words but the Armenian smelled so strongly of lavender water that it disturbed her computations.

The Armenian was obliged to relinquish his umbrella to open his sheepskin. 'Miracles for the miraculous,' he offered, 'consummation for the chaste!'

'What have you brought me?' said the Warden's Mother impatiently.

'The posterity of your Daughter,' began the jeweller again, struggling with a knot, 'deserves nothing but the best –'

The Warden's Daughter tried to imagine herself deserving the best, and failed again. So she concentrated on scooping the last of the jam from the jar.

'How much?' snorted the matriarch abruptly.

The Armenian fumbled, became flustered and, instead of stating his price, at that moment let all the papers drop out of his arms. He watched in dismay as they tumbled and rolled across the carpets in rustling silence.

At the same moment, a thread of rosy jam oozed between the fingers of the Warden's Daughter and plopped on to her thigh.

Drat, thought the Armenian jeweller, in Armenian.

Bother, thought the Warden's Daughter in silence.

Paper, gasped the Scribe. The breath of the phoenix, the fragrance of certitude! How could words survive such surfaces? The murmur of silk, the touch of eternity! How narrow was the wood pulp and the rag, how limited the straw! These rolls were like the houris of paradise, clear as a day of sudden thaw. His knees weakened at the sight of them across the floor.

'We live in a time of miracles!' the Armenian began, with renewed zeal.

'The miracle would be if people shut their mouths,' growled the old lady.

'And in an age of catastrophes,' continued the jeweller, unperturbed, as he planned his next strategic moment, '"there's more beneath ink than what we think!"'

The Warden's Mother swore an oath. A pox on babblers, she thought.

The jam had spread everywhere. The Warden's Daughter prayed the Scribe would not look up and see her.

But he had eyes only for the Armenian's papers. And as they tumbled at his feet, he began an inventory of all the loves and debts he had accumulated. Roll after roll spread over the floor, as relentless as the unfolding years; bolt after unravelling bolt laid his life bare. He remembered how his master's daughter had suffered ignominy when his letters to her were discovered, how her virtue lost all its market value after he had run away. The Scribe had nursed his own hurt pride for years, but it was only when these unrolling papers caused him to step beyond the confines of himself that he recalled the silent humiliations of the girl.

Forgery is one crime, denial is another, he thought, remembering the maiden in his dream. Her green song threatened because it demanded to be written down. He had to bear witness to that unmarried loveliness if he was to master the scribe's art of true servitude. Already he imagined his pen scoring those spaces. Already he saw the ink intent upon its enviable destination. He yearned to follow.

'I'll use the style of *shikaste*,' he thought, the broken writing that had liberated penmanship, 'I'll use a script that stretches letters to their limits!' Since this paper was limitless in its translucence, perhaps his manual could reveal the naked truth to all the world.

A spasm passed through the Warden's Daughter. The situation could not have been more terrible. Her cheeks blazed.

' "Wherever there's smoke, there's paper" sir!,' quipped the Armenian. 'They say the coffeehouse combusted spontaneously –!'

Like salamanders, thought the Scribe, as the papers licked the red carpets.

Like quilts on a bed, thought the dazed Warden, half-asleep.

Like a bolster, anguished the Warden's Daughter.

The Warden's Mother did not think because she was counting.

' "There's no faith worse than debt!" ' the Armenian was saying. His moment had come. 'You couldn't have a better deal!'

'Deals be damned!' the Warden's Mother erupted. 'That's enough.'

The Scribe's entrails melted, for eternity had slipped, green and unseen, between her calculations and a curse.

'Five *qerans*,' she pronounced curtly. 'No more, no less.'

'I offer bargain rates,' began the jeweller.

'Take it or leave it,' snapped Her Ladyship.

'I propose the highest quality at the lowest price,' he struggled.

'That's my first and last word,' she thundered.

'And is there nothing in between?' quavered the Armenian.

But the old woman did not hear him. 'Five *qerans* and an inventory before payment,' she repeated, signalling the Scribe to record it. He looked up, trembling.

And as he did so, tears welled in the eyes of the Warden's Daughter for the third time that day. The miracle had occurred, and the situation was unimaginable. The Scribe must think she was as fat as the bolsters in the tearoom, the bolsters with cherry-coloured patches at each end. And her sobs showered like petals through the screen.

The jeweller knew that there was no point in further bargaining. He had not anticipated customers who might be too distracted or too deaf to hear him. Even the treacherous secretary looked everywhere except in his direction. There was no alternative but to accept the ignominious deal.

But if the Scribe stared in all directions at that moment, it was only because he was looking for the incalculable roll of cellophane paper. He was not sure whether the old woman had lost count by mistake or had expected him to cheat the Armenian on her behalf, but in either case if this roll had survived her computations it could be no ordinary paper. It was certainly translucent enough to purify his motives, wide enough to hide his fraud; it was surely pure enough to show the naked truth to all the world.

But just as he was beginning to think his manual might become a poem, there was a commotion outside. The writing of the inventory was stopped and a messenger was ushered abruptly into the reception room.

The Russian foreigner was begging for sanctuary at the gates, he reported. He had fled from the Turk who claimed he had burned down the coffeehouse.

The matriarch rose to the ponderous possibility of her feet. Clapping her hands for the papers to be brought after her into the *anderoun*, she swayed out of the room, in waves. Payment, she intoned, would be indefinitely deferred.

And it was only as the maternal tide receded that the plaintive whimpers were heard in the *anderoun* above. The Scribe was not sure whether the bleating sound was coming from above his head or in his ear. The messenger was handing him a fold of paper. The foreigner had addressed a petition to the Warden, he whispered. But His Honour was staring so oddly – would the secretary care to oblige?

The Warden had assumed that the Armenian was trying to blackmail him; he thought the hints he had been dropping during the conversation revealed his knowledge of the Crown Prince's demands. And if he was staring oddly it was because he had been figuring out what he would have to pay the Armenian to keep his mouth shut about the Kurdish troops. While his Mother had been measuring the girth of her Granddaughter's virginity, he was calculating how much silence he could afford and had concluded that all this paper would prove astronomically expensive. But when he turned to bribe the man to hold his tongue, the jeweller had fled.

The Armenian had been appalled by the impact of that scrap of paper. When the messenger whispered in the Scribe's ear and the Scribe whispered in the Warden's ear, the consequence of these accumulated murmurs was thunderous. For as soon as he received the paper in his hands, the Khan of the Eastern Marches started sending everyone off to the citadel. He roared that the Russian should be conducted straight up the mountain for questioning. He barked at the Scribe to follow and make a full report of the proceedings. And he ordered the messenger to run up ahead and ensure that a ream of the Prisoner's paper would be ready for his arrival. It was clear to the jeweller that if he wanted to avoid having paper rammed in his throat, if he wanted to avoid incarceration in the citadel along with the rest of them, he would have to bid a hasty retreat. Since the unspoken extended beyond the boundaries of utterance, and his best remarks, like his prices, had remained inside his head, he backed hurriedly out of the room without a further word. He grabbed his shawls, stumbled through the courtyard, and ignored the Russian at the entrance of the palace as he ran pell-mell across the barrack square. The snow had stopped falling and there was the hint of a thaw in the air as he squelched through the gates and ploughed down to town through the drifts. It was a miracle that he had managed to escape, he told his wife.

His life had been preserved from heaven and earth and all that lay between them.

But despite his speedy return, her prophecies of gloom were confirmed. For to his dismay, the Armenian discovered that he had left his umbrella behind him.

15 MIRACLES

I t was not the white umbrella, abandoned downstairs, which caused the most conjectures that day. It was the slip of paper which the Scribe gave to the Warden.

His Mother did not hear where it had come from or who had sent it. But when she saw the Scribe handing it to her son she feared for her Granddaughter and decided to apply the paper prescription promptly.

The Warden's Daughter could not feel anything but pain. And so she accepted to be wrapped in paper, in order to absorb it.

As for the Warden, all he could register was that the Russian's petition was written on English paper. Here were conspiracies of international dimensions! His mind reeled with questions as his secretary whispered in his ear.

The Scribe was suggesting that he should test the surveyor's true intentions. In the past, when an Arabian chieftain wanted to gauge his servants' motives, he would question them and inscribe their answers on pieces of paper, he said. Then, according to ancient custom, each man was forced to eat his own words. All that was needed was enough paper to stuff down the man's throat. The quality was irrelevant.

The Warden heard his secretary through a dream.

'Perhaps you wish to interrogate the fellow up at the citadel, sir,' the Scribe was murmuring. 'The Prisoner has plenty of paper to spare for such purposes.'

The Warden almost snored. He barely registered his secretary's words and simply repeated them, to the terror of the Armenian. 'I wish to interrogate the fellow up at the citadel,' he said. For there was a limit to how much a man could endure.

*   *   *

The Russian had written his petition for a laissez-passer on the last scrap in his escritoire. All the rest of his reams had been burned. He had been writing when his oil lamp toppled over causing the fire in the coffeehouse. His ink had congealed, and he had been obliged to break the black ice in his ink-well in order to write. He was conjuring whorls and curls across the blurry page when sleep swooned over him.

'O Moon beyond the Mountain that oppresses me,' he arabesqued, and then paused, for his eyelids were drooping. The howling winds woke him. 'It has been some time now since your bright eye eclipsed all other eyes,' he wrote, and then, having read the quavering line over in the dim light of the oil lamp, he scratched it out hopelessly, licked the thin moustache on each side of his mouth, and began again.

The Russian had always prided himself on his handwriting. As a student, he tried to elongate his letters as far as the paper allowed, but although his grandmother thought this proved him eminently qualified for government office, his cousins were of a more critical bent. They were particularly critical when the old lady left him the sole inheritor

168

of her cherry orchards, for they held in low esteem the young man who had been born posthumously and raised frivolously by his sentimental grandparent. He was given to understand that he was no longer welcome to spend his summers in the family dacha, developing the art of illegibility and cultivating a rather disappointing moustache. Let him elongate his letters elsewhere, they said.

After proving his ineptitude in history and law, the Russian student discovered that elsewhere lay in the study of cartography. He may have lost the Parthian wars, but he was determined to ride in triumph through the Caucasus, and soon set his sights on surveying the wilds of Transoxania. It was during the winter ball season, and why Russian eyes should be turned from the wide circumference of hoop petticoats and fixed on such a cultural void was beyond his cousins' understanding. They expected these portentous vernations to shrivel by the spring and were greatly surprised, some time later, to learn that their relative had left his university apartments and was travelling south. Although they muttered of premature rottenness rather than maturity, the boy's resolve was distinguished, on paper at least, by the virtue of consistency. For his first letter, written in vegetal style, arrived soon after by diplomatic pouch from Tiflis, authorizing the sale of the orchards and requesting payments to be sent care of a certain Armenian, who would serve as his banker in the region. The letter also stated that if all contact failed in the coming months, his family could address themselves to the nearest Russian Mission, in order to retrieve his personal effects, his scientific records and, if possible, his remains. While most of his cousins noted how rapidly his legacy was being wasted on the delights of the theodolite and the extravagance of aneroid barometers, no one guessed that even while his instruments dangled over the high passes the young surveyor's heart had been already lost. Irretrievably lost.

'Divine Diana from whose wrist I fly,' the Russian wrote, unsteadily, 'permit me to return that I might climb still higher.' He paused and crossed out the words 'to return', hesitated, rewrote 'to return' and crossed out 'that I might climb still higher'. He blinked uncertainly. His mind was a delicate faculty and he had a fatal propensity to fall asleep while writing. 'Inspire me,' he wrote, 'to fly higher.'

Ever since the Georgian Envoy had offered to provide him with a laissez-passer if he went straight to the point and stated the facts exactly as they were, the Russian had struggled to be succinct, to chart his mental voids in clear black ink. But it was only as his paper dwindled that he confronted the terrors of brevity and truth. By the end of the summer he was reduced to buying the worst kind of straw for his specimens. He had submitted to even graver humiliation for rag, to draw his maps. But as long as he had no laissez-passer, languor still interposed its doodles.

'Were it not that your remembrance,' he wobbled, 'has kept me thus remote, I would entreat . . .' He struggled to keep his eyes open. 'I would request,' he scrawled, and crossed it out. 'I would beg,' he scribbled. 'Make a pledge which may.' His pen dawdled into a squiggle, petered into a doodle and finally dozed into a blot. He drifted for a few seconds before waking with a jerk as the wind whined. 'Which may not,' he rewrote. 'Dissuade future reunions. Dare I aspire.' He corrected this to 'dare I desire'. He crossed it out again and wrote, 'may I still dream'. But by then he had sagged irresistibly towards sleep. At the first snore his foot kicked the oil lamp through the gap of the floor-boards into the coffeehouse. Unaware of the wisps of smoke that festered, gathered force and burst into flames below him, the Russian snored on, his dreams wandering across the unexplored spaces of the beckoning page.

Although he had done all he could since coming to these regions, to resist the encroaching march of British red and Napoleonic green across lands destined for the imperial orange of the Tsars, the surveyor was much exercised by what constituted sufficient grounds for a duel. He had spilled much ink on the subject during his last year at the university and had concluded that given the precedent established by heroes of the time and national poets of the past, one needed, at the very least, sufficient paper. The daughter of the Minister recently appointed to the court of the Persian Shah had certainly given him grounds to think so. She had broken hearts with her boredom at the winter balls and he, for one, had been so smitten at the sight of her yawns that he had pursued her straight into the winter conservatory, an act which later cost him a legacy in paper. It also left him blinded, not only by his passions but by the unfortunate loss of his glasses, which cracked at the same instant as his heart.

'Pretty cuff-links!' she had said, eyeing them as she played idly with the tip of a fern. 'I like falcons.' He was speechless. 'Do you like hunting too?' she inquired vacantly. He was mute with adoration. 'I do,' she added and then, with a bored glance over his shoulder, she did it again, giving him the personal benefit of her entire submission to the involuntary impulse. He shivered with pleasure as he remembered the violence of it, the seizure of her shoulders, the surrender of her eyes, the heaving and gaping of her breasts and lips. The Russian dissolved, he was engulfed by her fathomless yawn. For he understood instinctively from it that she must love him.

'I adore hunting,' she sang, and the words widened wonderfully to receive him. 'Papa says that I can go hunting in Persia, with a falcon on my arm!'

The conciliatory ferns bending over his head seemed to dip down from paradise at her words. He could not help dipping his own head at that moment, to snatch a favour from her charming hand. She pulled it away immediately.

'How dare you take such liberties!' she pouted, and stamped her equally charming foot. 'Do go away,' she sulked deliciously. 'Go to the ends of the earth!'

She wanted him at the ends of the earth? It was prophecy and he had to fulfil it. She could brook no delay? Exquisite! He would most certainly obey.

Just then, a swaggering Cossack entered the conservatory. 'Where were you for the polka?' she yawned. 'I've been so bored!' But she cast a smouldering glance of petulance, or perhaps passion, behind her, as she swept away on the officer's arm.

That was when he realized how deep the game was, and how high the stakes. He understood then that she had accepted his devotion. But no one else must know it, least of all the Cossack. The barbarian's jealousy of their secret liaison led to the acquisition of sturdy, wire-rimmed spectacles in the days that followed. Because by then, the young man had fixed his gaze on more distant horizons.

For when the Minister's daughter accompanied her father to the Land of the Lion and the Sun, he followed. He became the falcon riding on her arm. Provisioning himself as a surveyor, courtesy of the Imperial Russian Geographical Society, he left in the wake of the diplomatic party and travelled south, determined to win her hand and his fame simultaneously. Before leaving he sent an elaborate map of Astrabad to the Cossack, announcing that he would answer him, with a duel, at the place whose name could either be read as 'the city of the star' or 'the town of the mule', depending on which interpretation one chose to follow. It was bruited about that he was a coward and had fled the capital. It was rumoured that his fortunes were not equal to his presumptions. It was whispered that he was as foolish as his grandmother.

No one, except his laundress who starched all his shirts prior to his departure, knew the real reasons for his going. The female yawn, he told her in a fit of extravagant trust, was a summons to the secret passes, the uncharted lands of mystic Lhasa; it had the power to draw a surveyor's soul to the white spaces in the Land of Snows. Startled by these disclosures, the laundress had replied, with a nervous simper, that she hoped, sir, it might extend to a liberal tip for the starched shirts. But she resisted his invitation to come up to his rooms, for she was an honest woman who preferred to keep her mouth shut, thank you. When she counted the meagre change he paid her, however, she removed five of the shirts and left him with a bunch of useless collars in revenge. There's a limit to what a woman can endure, after all.

The surveyor reached his own limits when the earthquake occurred the previous autumn. He had thought the Envoy had brought him his laissez-passer, and in his haste to take charge of his identity papers at last, he quite ignored the possibilities of incivility or death. But on crawling up to his room that night, he thought death had entered it before him. He thought someone was hovering there in the dusky light, standing before him, like a moth with folded wings. When the apparition vanished, he assumed he had been dreaming, and it was only some days after the earthquake that he found the sheet of paper on the floor. It was a single sheet, green in colour, a hand's span in size, and fathom-lessly blank. He had no idea where it came from. Most people told him that it was probably dropped by a thief, which was rather banal. The Turk believed he was under the observation of a passing spy, which was more inter-esting. The local Mullah said it might have been left there by a heretic or perhaps a passing traveller bringing supplies for the Prisoner at the citadel, but as far as the Russian was concerned, it was the death of his hopes for a laissez-passer. For by then he had realized his mistake.

On scrutinizing this mysterious sheet, which symbolized his limitations, the Russian had discovered it was of English manufacture. He did not know if it was worse to have followed directions to the wrong destination or be denied official papers once he was there, but he stuffed it into his escritoire and tried to ignore the memories of perfidious Albion it evoked. Since it was easier to contemplate human boredom than existential indifference, however, he asked the proprietor for the services of a prostitute after that, and paid the girl to yawn the whole night through.

But this solitary sheet of blank paper finally offered him a last chance of escape. After the fire at the coffeehouse, the piece of paper dropped in his room by some spy or thief or heretic or passing traveller by mistake was all the young Russian had left in his escritoire. And so he used it, as the Georgian had advised, to go straight to the point and ask the Warden directly for a laissez-passer.

*   *   *

Rumours about the Russian's paper rippled round the palace like wildfire. Not only was it green, but it was revolutionary, they said; it marked the turning of the times. No wonder the icicles were melting on the window panes that afternoon and dripping from the fretted balconies. Soon after the Armenian slithered down the mountain into the town and the Warden marched the Scribe and the Russian up to the citadel, their footprints grew cavernous around the gates. And by the time the news arrived that the last of the winter caravans had brought dispatches from Tabriz, the Charlatan's red ochre paint was running down the steaming walls, like sap in spring.

Despite these miracles, the women in the *anderoun* were not at first convinced that paper could affect the temperature. Even if it could absorb dreams, it was useless against the seasons, they hissed. No amount of paper could soak up stupidity either, they muttered, nudging each other to prise the stuffing out of the keyhole in the tearoom door. They ventured to suggest that Her Ladyship was out of her mind to think that cellophane could either stimulate or resist the onset of a girl's menses.

Even if there was a limit to miracles, however, there seemed to be none to catastrophes that day. Once the couriers arrived with the letters from the Crown Prince, the demise of the whole dynasty was written on Her Ladyship's face. Since the girl was not even fit for marriage, why cocoon her in illusions and wrap her in lies, sneered her aunts, ogling through the tearoom door. Why bother to bolster her in wallpaper, sniggered her cousins peering at the Hope of the Kurds under the portrait of Connubial Bliss. There should be a limit to wasting paper, after all.

But there seemed to be no limit to the Warden's Daughter. The volumes of paper unrolled from round her covered the tearoom floor. And the blurs and blots inscribed on them bore witness that these marks of womanhood were copies, merely, of the many ordeals she had passed before. Her reiterations were as deep as her silences. And although the women took turns to peep through the keyhole, although they sucked in their cheeks and licked their lips to press closer to the door, they only glimpsed at bits and pieces of the girl. They drooled at the soft dough of her, they gawped at her spongy sweetness, they gorged on her syrups and her flaky pastries, but the boundless humility of the Warden's Daughter resisted their facile interpretations.

Her Grandmother scrutinized each sheet she peeled, investigated each bolt she stripped from that elephantine body. And when the crinkling envelope was unrolled from round the girl, when each piece was unwound, its creases smoothed, its wrinkles spread flat across the carpets, the Warden Mother saw that the paper had been covered with a thousand cherry-red signs; it had been inscribed with a myriad ruby-tinged desires. It was embossed with crimson petals and scarlet peacocks all confirming the same truth. They revealed the future written indelibly on the past. They proved that ecstasy will lose its virtue when it is not shared. And they showed that the Hope of the Kurds had been stamped all over with the watermarks of love.

And since love is written in the mother tongue, which is a language that none can deny, the old woman stumbled to her swollen feet then, to embrace her Granddaughter. But whether it was too late or perhaps too soon for such a miracle, the girl shrank from the matriarch's mottled arms, and wrapped herself in silence.

She stood perfectly still in red rebellion, peeled naked in the middle of the carpet. She did not defend herself for the truth was so beautiful that it blazed all over her. She did not answer her Grandmother's questions or heed the women huddled behind the door. She suffered the perfect knowledge of herself under an immaculate veil of silence.

But though the bruises of maturity recall the aching scars of childhood, they can be mute from choice rather than from tyranny. Everything had changed for the Warden's Daughter since she had undergone the dignity of pain. Her situations sang in her, like crimson rain. She had no further need for the copy of her varnished self now that she could read her own original.

Slender as a river reed she stood, arced as a cypress, lilting as the breeze that loosed the trammels of her hair. Elegant and sinuous she stood, with her feet in perfect parallel among the wise hyacinths. Modest and impertinent she swayed, pressing her finger against her coral lips. The stuff of her robes was pale as gossamer as she danced among anemones; the breeze eddied like unspoken silk from round her throat as she sang. And the Scribe was playing music for her as he turned the pages of his book.

The Warden's Daughter longed to dance the whole book that the Scribe was reading. She yearned to sing the white writing through the black ink of his story. For while the right page of his music turned continuously, the left page never changed at all. Since the scope of her intent spanned heaven and earth and all that lay between them, she tossed her silken silence in the air and leaned towards him. And as she did so the Warden's Daughter saw her image glimmering in the mirror page.

The Scribe was reading her and no one knew it; he was watching her secret dance, which no one else could see! No one could guess that his gaze caressed her, as she swooned against the cypress, melted into the hyacinths, flowed into the river and dissolved in ecstasy towards him. No one realized when she stepped into his book and gave her loveliness to him alone, when she flattened herself inside the pages where only he might find her, when she let his

177

hand touch her, far from the reach of her Grandmother's yearning disappointments, far from her cousins' sticky fingers, and the mocking of the women through the whispering keyhole of the door.

16 PAPER DREAMS

T he Russian surveyor stood perfectly still before the
Warden up at the citadel. He did not protest his
innocence or defend his honour, for the truth was so banal
that it could not be believed. He simply bowed his head
and prayed for a laissez-passer as the Scribe's nail crawled
across the paper.

Before the official interrogation began on the Prisoner's
paper, the Scribe had been instructed to make a new entry
in the Warden's official register and record the coffeehouse
fire as an official catastrophe. Many defined it as a miracle,
but this ambiguity escaped the blackened nail.

There was no record either, in the Warden's register, of
the dream of the Russian youth. For when he had fallen
asleep writing his last letter, that night in the coffeehouse,
he had dreamed that he was in the King's pavilion, carrying
a falcon on his arm. He had been waiting for the hunt to
begin, but when the horn began to blow he found to his
dismay that he himself had become the prey and all his
letters were fluttering to the ground like plump partridges.
To add to his confusion the falcon on his arm began to
yawn and he was so threatened by the fierce immensity of it
that he woke, choking with the smoke, and found himself

running out of his dream and the coffeehouse at the same instant, all the way up to the palace on the hill. By the time he reached the citadel that afternoon, he was simply grateful to be standing still.

Despite his chronic exhaustion, the Warden noted a discrepancy between the robust rumours he had been hearing about the foreigner all these months and the miserable creature before him. But he was not sure whether lack of evidence or sleep made the young man's neck so thin, his eyes so dim, and his moustache so limp. He had every intention of imposing customs duties on the foreigner, however. Taxes were a lucrative source of revenue and since his half-brother took good advantage of them, the Warden was determined to demand tariffs from the young man in exchange for a laissez-passer. Whether or not he was a smuggler or a spy, it was obvious that he was withholding vital information, for he hardly spoke. The Warden had witnessed drought and plague, earthquake and fire in town that year and the last thing he wanted now was a conspiracy of silence. History was filled with rebellions caused by misapplied reticence. If he was starved, let him eat his own words, he thought.

There was a note of desperation in the barking of the dogs that warned the young man against words, however. The hollow-eyed Warden looked straight through him during the tedious interrogation and his secretary, too, refused to meet his eye and seemed not to listen to anything being said. There was an unpropitious detachment about the manner in which his hand moved across the rasping page that suggested there was no relationship between what he wrote and what he heard. His thumb nail, dipped in ink, seemed to be governed by a dangerous lack of accountability. It was split at the tip and blackened with gall. The Russian had never seen anything like it.

When he was told to identify himself for the chancery records, the surveyor preferred not to risk a long speech, therefore. He feared his words might tear the page. He had lost everything: all his specimens, his starched shirts, his illusions and his maps. But he did not admit to wasting his inheritance or having been reduced to penury. He begged the Khan of the Eastern Marches to extend him hospitality for one night and give him a laissez-passer to travel to the capital at the earliest opportunity. But he did not add with what dread he would address himself at the Russian Legation; he did not say his love was unrequited, his heart broken.

The Warden was too tired to do anything but follow instructions. The foreigner surveyor could leave the town with the couriers at dawn, he grunted, and guards would accompany him as far as the crossing at Julfa. From there he would be alone, with a laissez-passer to ensure safe passage beyond the boundaries of the Marches. But his guest would remain at the citadel under strict guard that night, slurred the Warden, because the Turk had proven dangerous to foreign agents in the past. He would be immured in solitude until the truth of his statements could be verified. He was not told by what means this would be ensured.

The deeper the dungeon, the truer it was, averred the Russian stoically.

The Warden suspected his acquiescence. He ordered the Scribe to write the laissez-passer on the sheets of chancery paper that remained, and decided that the fellow should swallow the Prisoner's paper blank. The paucity of his answers would not amount to sufficient stuffing anyway, and the Khan wished to verify by this means if the Russian was also responsible for the Prisoner's escapes. He murmured to the Scribe that the laissez-passer need not offer full protection to the bearer: just the minimum coverage for the region under his surveillance. He need not have taken the precaution of murmuring, for a murder over the borders often passes unnoticed.

He was waiting to sign the document when there was a clatter of hooves and shouts in the courtyard. A guard entered the citadel in a cloud of steam and respect.

He reported breathlessly that the last winter caravans had arrived that morning and that the couriers had delivered letters at the palace soon after His Honour's departure. He begged to inform the Warden that one of the letters bore the seal of the Crown Prince. A royal progress was being prepared in Tabriz. The Prince was planning to arrive on these frontiers with the first spring thaws, he said.

There was a pause during which the dogs howled and the shoulders of the Guard gradually sagged. The Scribe's nail scratched. The Warden said nothing.

The Warden's Mother, said the Guard hesitantly, had summoned His Honour to the palace immediately. He did not add with what wrath she summoned. He did not say with what fury she had crumpled the paper from Tabriz or what dreadful rustlings and cracklings had been heard through the walls of the *anderoun* afterwards.

The Guard waited, as the nail of the Scribe continued to scratch. Water dripped from the lintel and the dogs lamented. The Warden still said nothing.

Her Ladyship was making travel plans, murmured the Guard, fixing his eyes miserably to the ground. He dared not mention that new secretaries appointed by the Prime Minister, who everyone knew were spies, had also arrived with the caravan.

After another pause, the Scribe dipped his thumb in gall and continued to scribble the last line of the laissez-passer. As the document came to a close, the Warden pulled the paper away from under his secretary's thumb a fraction too soon.

And botched the signature. The blot spread.

'Tell them to saddle my horse,' he mumbled, and was about to place his seal over the mistake when the wax spilled and seeped through the page. The last of chancery papers was spoiled and the laissez-passer was ruined. 'Use the Prisoner's paper to copy another,' said the Warden dully, and then sleepwalked into the stables.

As he mounted his nightmare to ride away, the Khan of the Eastern Marches finally understood what was at the root of his troubles. He realized who was the mastermind behind this paper plot. It had been his Mother all along! He had to hurry before she called the Kurds to raid. He had to stop her rousing the troops in mutiny against him. He knew that once she left, the Prisoner would slip out of his control completely. There was no time to lose! And he rode through the gates of his dreams on the spurs of slumber all the way down the slope. But he forgot to tell the guards, before he left, to ram the ream of the Prisoner's paper down the Russian's throat.

*　　*　　*

The Scribe was marooned in the citadel, waiting for the Prisoner's paper.

Why was it taking so long to come?

The Guard probably had to fight his way through reams of paper, he thought, that had been delivered to the Prisoner all through the summer, autumn and the winter seasons. Paper had been brought to this citadel from far and wide. The very walls revealed disturbing glimmers, which had they not been scraps of paper might have been the bones of prisoners immured alive. The dungeons were doubtless filled with folios of it, the corridors crammed with quires. This massive four-towered citadel, hallucinated the Scribe, is made of paper delivered to the Prisoner. But only the drips from the lintel, the snivels of the Russian, betrayed the secrets of the stones.

Despite the change in his appearance, the Russian surveyor remembered the slanting figure he had encountered the previous summer. The last time they had met, this wandering scholar had been frayed at the wrist and cringing; now he was a chancery official, dressed in fine wool with a waistcoat of embroidered silk. He used to be bare-headed but was now crowned by a tall lambskin hat. His beard was carefully trimmed and perfumed and he wore boots with fashionable, pointed toes. He was, to all outward appearances, very different from his original.

'My life for yours, sir!' began the Russian, uncertainly.

The Scribe had lost the art of response in his loneliness.

The Russian tried again. 'I believe you were kind enough to provide me with some straw paper at the mosque last summer?' he hazarded.

The Scribe winced at the recollection.

'Or maybe I had the pleasure of your acquaintance in the company of His Honour the Envoy down at the coffee-house?' inquired the Russian hopefully.

The Scribe did not deny or confirm this possibility.

'I'm much obliged to the royal Envoy,' remarked the other with a wistful sigh. 'I owe him a debt of life, as I am a gentleman.'

He was ready to offer further confidences but the Scribe cut him short.

'His Honour is dead,' he said, hating the sound of his own voice.

The lintel dripped, the icicles streamed their indistinguishable drivel down the walls. A grave yawned between the two men as dogs barked and soldiers argued in the garrisons, their muffled voices merging in the mist. The Russian fell silent. The Scribe rubbed his palms together briskly and fixed his eyes on the open door.

The couriers who had arrived from Tabriz that day had not been certain of the cause although they brought news of the Georgian's demise. He had either been poisoned in the *anderoun* on his return to court or had taken his own life, apparently. According to one story, he had dressed himself in ceremonial robes and killed himself to escape public shame, like the Chinese eunuch who had invented paper and was then condemned for committing forgery. According to another, he had fled from court and joined a fanatical sect on the Russian borders, which was just as bad.

'His Honour was very kind to me,' said the Russian suddenly.

The Scribe wondered whether ignorance or forgiveness endured longer. As the Russian babbled on about his laissez-passer, and how the Envoy had promised to help him acquire it, and how he had advised him to go straight to the point and ask the Warden for it so many months ago, time stretched to limits of eternity for the Scribe. Time ripped and tore to shreds; it was macerated. Time was soaked in lime and beaten to pulp and strained and pressed thin. Time shrivelled and dried, waiting for paper.

'I've been trapped without papers, you see!' the young man was saying. 'They're my passport to freedom, my proof of integrity. When people read them I'll have right of passage. They're worth more than a map to me, sir,' he concluded.

'No one can read around here anyway,' interrupted the Scribe.

'But everyone speaks so many languages,' marvelled the other. And was ready to name them. 'Kurdish, Turkish, Persian, Armenian, Georgian, Russian,' he sang.

'And they're illiterate in all of them,' said the Scribe bluntly.

'So am I, sir,' said the Russian, lifting his hands in a gesture of resignation.

The Scribe could not endure the Russian's sincerity; it touched him to the quick. He sensed new meanings inscribed invisibly upon time, like a watermark of immortality, in the other man's open palms.

'If you can't read it, what's the use of a laissez-passer?' he retorted.

The Russian bowed humbly; the Scribe could hardly bear to look at him.

'I mean, what's the point of having identity papers if you don't know what they say?' he struggled.

The question expanded as the two men shrank from each other into silence.

Since it was painful for the Russian to admit that he had been supplying himself with meanings for months, he held his tongue. Words were only worth anything if one knew what they meant. It was disturbing to consider that his life depended on a piece of paper which neither he nor anyone else could actually read.

Since it was painful for the Scribe to admit that he would be writing something that had no meaning, he had no desire to speak either. It was futile to write what would never be understood. Why waste the Prisoner's paper on such a worthless document? How much paper had he already squandered, how many reams wasted since he had come to these frontiers! Fields of straw reduced to fake cures for the Charlatan and folios of obfuscation forfeited for the Mullah's will. Reams of rags ripped off the backs of shivering wretches for the sake of forgeries he had committed on the chancery paper. Landslides prescribed by the Envoy, snow drifts dictated by the Warden, the flurries of delay and distortion sent to the Crown Prince throughout the winter season. And most recently, how many mighty forests he had hacked to pulp for Her Ladyship. All the paper of the world reproached him for wasting it: false inventories, fraudulent contracts, unpaid promissory notes and fathomless debts. And was he now obliged to waste the Prisoner's paper too?

But perhaps the season of fulfilment had finally come round. He had passed through all the gates in town and stood on the threshold of the last frontier. Ever since the Armenian's bulk paper had cracked the confines of his mind that day, he had begun to ponder truths that had eluded him before. He had realized that there was no limit to alternatives, no end to interpretations. What if the heart of his master's Daughter had been broken? What if the letters he had written for her had been stolen? What if she had loved him long before he wrote to her of love? How many futures had been lost by confining his definitions of the past! How far the present stretched beyond his seeing!

Only the Prisoner's paper could reflect such multiple possibilities.

This paper was more precious than wood pulp, more rare than rags or silk, he thought. It contained infinite possibilities of danger and of beauty in its unblemished surfaces. It threatened social chaos and perturbed political desires precisely because it promised the fulfilment of impossible dreams. It caused terror in every church and dread among the clergy just because it was recognized by heretics of every denomination. It reflected an eternal, living scroll of light which threatened all the scribal traditions and commanded them at the same time. It bore the watermark of the human soul, the Scribe realized, because its sincerity was proof against all counterfeit.

I could write what I wanted on it and no one would be any the wiser, thought the Scribe with a deep, cold breath.

He wrapped his arms round himself, and shivered. The Warden had probably forgotten about the foreigner already. He had far more to worry about than what was written in a laissez-passer. Trouble had been brewing in the *anderoun* all morning, and now, it seemed, the Crown Prince was on his way to these borders. The days of the Khan were probably numbered and the Eastern Marches would soon pass into other hands. This paper need not attest to anything but the Russian's faith in it.

The Scribe realized that no one was dictating this laissez-passer. The paper of the Prisoner was a luminous door leading him towards infinity; it beckoned him to follow, through the labyrinth of the citadel, like an unending scroll that rolled into the spaces of eternity. He could go wherever he desired through this bright screen, cross whatever boundaries he wished, pass into other worlds. The possibilities shimmered before him. They encompassed his dreams. They included his poem!

He heard the footsteps approaching then. And as the door was opened, the Scribe saw that the guard was not alone. The Prisoner's amanuensis was with him.

17 THE OFFER

T he Scribe recognized the Persian amanuensis immediately, though he was thinner than before. Winter in
this desolate spot had not been kind to him. His face was
gaunt, the sockets of his eyes sunk deep, but whether this
was due to the extremities of hunger or submission was
uncertain. The exercise of acquiescence lent itself to complex interpretations but whichever one had marked this
man had made him more than a copy of his former self.
The air of authenticity he bore depended on nothing so
little as his material well-being. Despite the unseasonable
weather, he was still dressed in the same thin, cotton shift,
the same shabby *aba*, but seemed inured to the cold. His
knuckles were chapped and bleeding and he was carrying a
ream of paper in his arms. The Scribe's throat tightened at
the sight of it.

'Your paper, sir,' said the Persian, dislodging time. The
dogs stopped barking.

Since they had had some previous acquaintance, he had
been permitted to bring the supplies in person, he continued, inclining his head towards the source of the con-
cession. His manner suggested that if he had no right to this
liberty he would assume the blame for having taken it, but

if the presumption were permitted, credit for the gesture could go to the Guard.

In the past, the Scribe had registered self-righteousness in the space between these possibilities, but now he found only the traces of humility. Before, he thought something was being taken from him but at this moment he felt himself the beneficiary. He was flooded with shame and gratitude simultaneously; he had an insane desire to greet the other with an embrace, in the manner of scribes, and to flee from him at the same instant. The gulf between them was immense. There was an absurdity in being so well shod in his expectations, so denuded of their fulfilment. It was ridiculous to be wearing these ostentatious chancery clothes in front of a threadbare copyist. Seasons had passed since their first meeting, the basil leaf had withered and withdrawn into a sleeve of snow. But the paper was alive!

'The Warden's orders,' he said. He was inarticulate, unable to tear his eyes away from the other man's hands.

'You provided me with supplies at his dictate too, sir,' said the Persian delicately. 'And I've been in your debt ever since, but I didn't forget my promise.'

Blank paper, it seemed, could also fulfil prophecies, but the Scribe brushed aside the awkward recollection. It reminded him of a promised voice, which threatened fulfilment, of a dream of his heart singing. He muttered that there was no chancery paper left at the citadel; no wood pulp, no rag, not even any straw. 'Which, as you know, is useless,' he concluded.

'In your hands, sir,' returned the other, 'no paper can be useless.' It was one of those sententious exchanges typical of scribes. His head was stuffed with such phrases. No paper is false if the scribe is true. No ink is spilled if it makes you think. A poet is born between each line. But what if the scribe was false, the ink frozen and the poem dead, he wondered, his cheeks burning. What if he was a mere copyist of history, unqualified to write the future?

'There is more, if this is not enough for your needs,' said the Persian.

The paper was almost more than he could bear. The Scribe stared at it; he had to set some limits to his needs lest they crack the walls of reason.

'You will need no burnisher with this, sir,' said the Persian. 'The surface is like a mirror.'

He offered his professional advice with the same air of quiet detachment with which he was stacking the paper against the wall, on the Guard's instructions. 'You need no sizing, either, to sustain the reed. The bite is very smooth and the touch of a finger sufficient.'

He was referring to the point of contact between the pen tip and the page, that undivulged point which made all the difference between accuracy and error. The Scribe lowered his eyes from the innumerable times he had abused the difference. How could the pen caress a page with both freedom and chastity? What art or perhaps science could summon a response from the paper to protect it from insincerity? But before he could register remorse, the Russian began a round of jolly greetings with the Guard. It was difficult, under his vapid chatter, for the Scribe to concentrate on the questions of the Persian.

'Do you wish for an assay, sir?' the amanuensis was saying with deference.

'No,' said the Scribe hurriedly. The last thing he wanted to do was to demonstrate his skill or lack of it before this knowing secretary and in the presence of an inquisitive foreigner.

'But may I ask, sir, which of the scripts you command?' continued the other. It was the usual query between those of his profession but the Scribe shrank from answering him.

'I submit to them all,' he muttered with reluctance. He had no wish to expose his mediocrities, for the script revealed the man, according to the manual.

'But in which,' persisted the Persian, 'do you excel?'

'I claim excellence in none,' replied the Scribe hurriedly, for, to excel in a script, he would have to see the word he had already written while envisaging the one he had not; he would have to be able to write and erase at the same instant. His mind would have to become as elastic as the chastity he had lost, combining contradictions on the page that had defeated him in life. Who but a houri of paradise could be forever faithful to the original and a unique creation at the same time? The Scribe could barely conceive of such paradoxes. Besides, his attention had been distracted at that moment. The Russian was showing marked interest in the Prisoner's paper.

'You may want to test the quality of response, perhaps,' said the Persian. 'The texture of the paper will tell you everything.' For it was well known among calligraphers that if the first stroke of the pen asked the right question, the paper itself would offer the correct answer. The Scribe did not wish to think of the right question or the correct answer just then. He was sure the quality was sufficient for a laissez-passer. He was not concerned if response were granted or denied, either. He wished only to take possession of the paper. Now.

'The gentleman,' he said lamely, 'requires travel documents.'

He did not add that paper could only grant a man the right of passage into other worlds if he had already crossed all the boundaries of this one. Travel documents were of little value to one already in possession of freedom.

The thought may have struck the Russian too. 'As I am a gentleman, I don't think I need travel documents!' he said abruptly. It was a bolt out of the blue.

The Scribe jerked round, in alarm. The fellow was examining the paper closely.

'My life for yours, sir!' he said, looking up. 'Your services will not be necessary!' His incandescent eyes, dazzling behind their lenses, supplied the only light in the room.

The secretary hesitated at his task, and the Guard stared at the foreigner suspiciously. But the Russian beamed at them. He had been unable to follow the ornate conversation taking place between the two Persians. And his greeting of the Guard did not extend beyond the boundaries of convention. But when he took off his grubby spectacles and looked closely at the pile of paper, everything became clear. 'On my honour, it's very true! If a laissez-passer can't be read, it's hardly worth the writing!' he said earnestly. 'So I'll do just as the royal Envoy advised!' He would travel to the capital directly, and address himself to the Minister without any intermediaries. Love had no need for words when the heart was its own map. He could see this clearly as he lifted the paper up against the light.

'Blank paper will be the test of my integrity!' he crowed.

The Scribe's heart missed a beat. He was about to leap across the room and ram the sheet down the fellow's throat for his presumption, when suddenly all the remaining papers slipped out of the hands of the Persian amanuensis. They dropped, scattering, to the ground; fluttered like petals; they rustled faintly, tinkled softly, like the sound of distant camel bells.

The Scribe gasped. He had to gather them quickly; he had to gather them all! And it was only when he fell involuntarily to his knees and started snatching the sheets away from the astonished Russian, it was only when the Guard, with an unnecessarily officious gesture, stepped between him and the foreigner who was also trying to pick up the pieces from the floor, that the Scribe noticed the secretary was laughing.

'It's only paper!' the Persian said. But there was no mockery in his tone. His face was aglow with patience and his words were sweet enough to attract the flies. And though the Scribe did not understand their full significance, he sensed the generosity in them immediately, and drew back abashed. The paper was unlimited; it surpassed the frontiers of possession. The Russian could have what he wanted and there would always be more where that came from. But above all, if his dreams could wait for such paper, with faith and without expectation, through countless seasons and for centuries, they too would never be owned. He was not only indebted to the Prisoner but to the patience of his amanuensis, for such boundless magnanimity. The debt had been repaid, he realized, a hundred-fold.

'I regret,' said the Persian, as the Guard signalled their departure, 'that I had no opportunity to see your penmanship, sir.'

It suddenly occurred to the Scribe that he had not only shown avidity of spirit, but had betrayed professional discourtesy towards this brother; he had omitted to reverse the other man's request, in the customary manner, and ask to see his work. He had missed a unique opportunity, lost the chance of seeing the work of a master in the mirror of his amanuensis.

'The loss is mine,' he began, starkly aware of the truth of his own words.

'As the gain would have been my privilege,' echoed the Persian with a smile.

He speaks by the book, thought the Scribe, but reads my heart. The old words seemed to stretch towards new intentions in the mouth of the other; the hypocritical phrases became luminous with sincerity. It was hard to see if mere courtesy or a more penetrating light shone in the Persian's eyes. The Scribe was at the point of tears. He pressed a finger to his lips and whispered, 'Peace! Peace!' for there was nothing more to say.

As they turned to go, he saw the Persian was extending to him, once again, the old ironic gesture of farewell. But this time he responded, with all his heart. He raised his fingers briefly to his forehead, pressed his hand to his breast, and bowed. It was the sign of faithfulness, of submission to the original, of a true scribe.

And so the brothers parted.

The shuffle of steps receded down the stone corridors of the citadel. The Russian subsided in his corner beside the brazier with a strange air of calm, and the Scribe settled his beating heart beside the precious paper. Silence seeped back into the cell.

Night owls began to hoot in the citadel. The sun had set and twilight deepened. And as the Scribe finally lifted the paper towards him, his shame, his anger and regret evaporated in surprise. For in the year of revolutions, during a late winter evening, on the frontiers of uncertain empires between changing times, he discovered, to his astonishment, that the Prisoner's paper was not blank at all. Peering at the page more closely in the brazier's light, he saw with disbelief that it was covered all over with writing!

18 READING

He called for an oil lamp, for the cell had grown too dark to see and the fire flickered too faint and too far for reading.

His head was reeling.

The last thing he had expected was to find the paper had already been used. He was dismayed. He was shocked, and then he was outraged. In the end he was invaded by haunting doubts. Was it possible that the Prisoner's paper was thick with words, covered with writing, scribbled with taunting calligraphy?

At first, he wanted to thrust the entire ream into the brazier and set it ablaze. Then he considered the consequences. It would only lead to misunderstandings. The guards would come. The Russian would not understand. Perhaps he would think the Scribe was burning his laissez-passer and that would create complications. So he did nothing.

Then he determined to summon the Persian secretary back. He wanted to accuse him of cheating and fraud, to insist on recompense, to order a replacement of the ream. And then he considered the practicalities. Could he justify his demands? What if he were mistaken? Shouldn't

he first double-check the paper in better light? So he said
nothing.

Briefly, he considered abandoning the whole affair. He
was ready, at that moment, to leave not only the citadel,
but the chancery too. He wanted to flee from the town. But
after some consideration, he realized that this would be
foolhardy. Darkness had fallen and the Kurdish guards
would be more inclined to ambush him than to provide
protection at such an hour. He was, in effect, imprisoned
for the night. And so he simply waited for the light.

The silence deepened in the cell. The Russian was
disinclined and the Scribe unable to speak. After some
time, a guard returned, without a lamp but with a samovar
for tea. Another followed with graceless rice on whose
glutinous surface was written the tale of the absence of
women in the garrison kitchens. The Scribe refused all
offers of food and drink and simply repeated his request.
But it seemed an oil lamp was not something easily acquired in the citadel. It was long in coming. And although
he struggled to decipher the paper in the growing gloom,
straining his eyes in the uncertain firelight, the room soon
grew too dark to see his hand or remember his indignation.
So he leaned back, stunned. And waited.

Night grew absolute. The dogs in the courtyard appeared
to have forgotten they were dogs and the soldiers abandoned all identity. Even the Russian ceased to snore. The
Scribe's feet were frozen. He heard the wings of an owl; he
counted the pulse of the dripping eaves; he only existed
because of the bones of the bricks pressed against his spine.

It was in order to ascertain if he were still alive that he
reached out towards the Prisoner's paper. It lay waiting in
the dark by his side, within an arm's length, a hand's span.
And even as he touched the ream, it seemed to glow at his

finger's tip; even as he teased the corners, tested the edges, caressed the surface beneath his palm, he realized with amazement that this paper appeared to be shining with an inner light. It glimmered with a strange, ethereal brightness, so luminous that the cell jumped to life and his shadow rose to meet it.

The Scribe knew then that all his dreams lay buried in the Prisoner's paper. They had been separated and scattered but had now reunited and combined in this paper, and were one.

But they had two sides – male and female, recto and verso, like a prophecy and its fulfilment – despite which there was no need to turn them over. The Scribe saw that there was no front or back to his dreams. Their binary configurations revealed the same truth, whether perceived sleeping or recalled awake, no matter which way you looked at them.

And, moreover, they had three textures, for there were dreams in which the body groped, dreams in which the mind wandered, and some dreams where the spirit soared. But despite these varied interpretations, their different surfaces required no sizing. The texture of the Prisoner's paper was mirror-smooth, needed no polishing.

Every dream, too, was moulded in four-fold silence, framed on four sides by the limits of human utterance. The dreams of this life stretched as far as the east; the equinoxes of the next were bound in by the west; the withholding and releasing silences lay to the north and south respectively. But within these frontiers lay the infinite pages of creation. The Prisoner's paper was limitless and scrolled forever beneath his thumb. It needed no trimming as it rolled ever onwards through the unutterable and unspeakable seasons.

Finally, there were five shades of meaning to his dreams, covering the full spectrum of a rainbow, springing unpossessed from whiteness and returning to it, unpossessing. For the Prisoner's paper could summon all the books of creation at a stroke and could just as easily erase them. And all these interlocking covenants lay in an arc beneath his fingertips, from the pale gold of justice to the purple of pure mercy, from the azure of detachment to the crimson of desire. At the point of perfect equilibrium, at the precarious centre of the prism, his dreams were of the rarest green. The colour of faith lay in the heart of the Prisoner's paper, and required courage if it was to be touched with the ordinary reeds of living. It lay bathed by its own light, anticipating nothing, detached from everything and threatening all.

There was no oil lamp available in the citadel, the Guard said roughly, stepping out of the night beyond the door. He carried a pale circle between his thumb and palm. This candle was all that could be spared, he said, and made it clear that he had no intention of losing sleep on further indulgences. The Scribe accepted the stub gratefully, despite the fact that he barely had any need for it now. He shielded the flame with his hand, for the taper was as fragile as hope, the wax as brief as friendship, and expressed his thanks to the Guard, with a full heart and a purse. The man gaped at the coins in his palm and stumbled out in a dream, with barely a glance at the snoring Russian huddled in the shadows of the cell.

The flame warmed the chilly walls and crumbling bricks around the Scribe. It summoned the hidden words to the surface of the Prisoner's paper. The calligraphy of the heart rose towards him, like steam on a mirror, like breath on ice. The Prisoner's paper chanted faintly as he lifted the ream to his lap. He smoothed away the dot of a winter fly, wiped the tablet of his thoughts clean and began to read.

*   *   *

Blank paper tests a scribe's integrity.
Written paper proves a scribe's fidelity.
Between the two lie all the dreams of life and death,
For in the space between the words a scribe defines his
*   faith.*

It was easy to miss the point because there were no dots to play with; it was easy to lose direction because there were no lines. The numerology of each letter hardly sufficed the sum of their syllables, and yet he could see that words must exist before they could be written down. For the page had been inscribed with a five-lettered calligram depicting a human hand.

If a scribe smells the paper at the start of the day's work,
his ink may flow well but he will be inclined towards
*   self-indulgence.*
If a scribe runs his fingers along the edge of the paper
*   before approaching its surface,*
his ink will clog and he will look for short cuts to
*   perfection.*
If he tests the fibres in the borders of a sheet before
*   trimming them,*
he is a reader of perimeters and will do no more nor less
*   than is required of him.*
For in the space between the words a scribe defines his
*   faith.*

The Scribe's first dream was about desire. The initial letter of the calligram was precarious in its contradictions. It revealed the curve of his right thumb, open at the palm and ready to receive, but it concealed his hooded nail, wrapped in a mantle, hidden in a sleeve. This letter was associated with mirrors and contained the number of danger days after childbirth, feast days after marriage and mourning days after death. It reminded him of that moment in the cherry orchards of life when a man realizes that he has done nothing and has everything left to do. A scribe could see what he wanted in such dreams as these.

If a scribe presses the dry reed in a downward stroke to
trace the nib on the chain lines before dipping his pen in
  ink,
he is not to be trusted among women.
If a scribe smooths the paper with the heel of his palm
  after burnishing it,
he may be inclined to extend his interests beyond his
  prerogatives.
For a scribe's faith must be defined between his words.

The Scribe's second dream was about fear and he hesitated at the sight of it, poised like a falcon over the page. He was uncertain how to read this letter of the alphabet which, like an index finger, showed him the way and sounded the warning simultaneously. It required one call only for the hunt, one echo only of the horn, to indicate its numerical worth. But although it was raised aloft like the all-sufficing cypress on the shining tablet of the spirit, its character inclined downward on the bare surface of human flesh, and followed the crude mandate of his insistent self. The associations of this dream, rubbing the foreskin of desire, made him blush with shame. A scribe could see what he feared most in dreams such as these.

The space on the page shows how far the scribe is
vulnerable to bribery.
The stress on the first impress shows how far a scribe can
be trusted.
The steadiness of a curve radiating from the pivot of the
wrist
shows whether or not a scribe is serving more than one
master.
A swerve at the end of a line is the sign of a scribe's
overweening ambition.
For a scribe defines his faith on the empty page.

He had reached the lull point of no return when neither pressing on nor going back seemed possible. He had come to the space between places in the no-man's-land between the words. And there, he saw his third dream brimful with its own beautiful emptiness. It floated like a split heart over the mountains, reflecting the moon like an unborn prayer. Its character dissolved selflessly, like the breath of white writing, and its vulnerability was like the marriage between jasper and pearl. This letter indicated the middle finger, at the centre of the calligram, and its number coincided with that of the pentacle. A scribe could either see what others saw or search for what no one else could see in dreams such as these.

Between the compass points of paper lies proof of a scribe's
capacity.
Between his work's perfection and its defects lies the scope
of his intent.

The Scribe's fourth dream was governed by the ring finger of his hand and contained the sum of all things and none. Its calligraphy recalled the cynicism of ceramics in the face of tumbling towers; it tossed aside the upward stroke of the character like the veil of an impatient virgin. The letter associated with this dream symbolized the scribal profession but its number was worldly and lent itself to easy calculations. It is enough to spread a coating of ignorance over one's spiritual nakedness, thought the Scribe. Such dreams as these pocketed counterfeit values under the craft of pride.

If the final work is sloppy, filled with orthographical errors, stained with smears, rendered in a derivative script, blotted by poor penmanship and breathless with lack of space, the scribe should be sent to the stables or simply promoted in the chancery.
If a finished copy is flawless, he may prove to be a dangerous forger and a thief because his faith can only be defined between the words.

The Scribe's fifth dream was symbolized by the last finger of his hand. Its number was associated with the six sides – above, below, before, behind, to the right and to the left – and since true protection extended beyond mere words, this dream breathed between them all. If he brought the page close to the candle, the letter reflected crimson fire. But if he held it far enough away, he could read pure light inscribed across the page. The Scribe knew from the curve of the letter, the last curl of this calligram, that should he ever succeed in copying it accurately, the eyes of the faithful would overflow with joy then, and he would weep with them, holding a lingering finger to his lips to whisper, 'Peace! Peace!'

If a scribe bends low to smell his paper at the end of a
day's work,
it may either be because his pride anticipates the very
flies,
or because he is a man of consummate humility.
Paper is where a scribe might prove his faith.

He read the Prisoner's paper to the end but had recognized this hand from the beginning. It was the manual for scribes written in the old way, on paper that was forever new. It was a faithful copy of his lost loves and dreams that was as radiant as the original. He realized then that the human soul must finally know submission, like any paper worthy of the name, for what had been inscribed here, on the Prisoner's paper, was written already with the ink of light on the tablet of his spirit.

And the paper was dancing for him in the flickering shadows, like a maiden. The paper was singing to him in the mirror of his dreams. And as his fingers caressed this girl of unmarried loveliness, blades of joy broke though him, hyacinths rose in his hands. As he pressed his lips against her cheeks, unspoken birds leaped in his throat and tossed like burnished falcons in the cypress skies. Although he knew he might be required to erase himself entirely in order to receive this sacrifice, he wept with gratitude as he embraced it. He could not bear that such innocence should give herself to him in vain.

There were no words for how he kissed the paper, no marks for where to trace his tongue, no sign for why these imprints were left on his mind. He was obliged to close his eyes against the dark dependence of his ink to see a breath of certitude had passed and left its signature for him to find. No one dictated what to write then, for his prayers were there.

'I shall copy them,' he thought. 'I shall inscribe them faithfully, in my own hand!'

His writing materials were laid before him. His ink gleamed ready, deepened with myrrh, and his thumb was ripe for the script of the living. So he dipped it, pressed down to release the Prisoner from the paper, and began to write.

It was a catastrophe, whichever way you looked at it. Or a miracle.

SPIRIT PAPER

Some wit of old, such wits of old there were,
Whose hints show'd meaning, whose allusions, care,
By one brave stroke, to mark all human kind
Call'd clear blank paper every infant mind;
When still, as op'ning sense her dictates wrote
Fair virtue put a seal, or vice a blot . . .

Various the papers, various wants produce
The wants of fashion, elegance and use.
Men are as various: and if right I scan
Each sort of paper represents some man . . .

Ascribed to Dr Benjamin Franklin, 1797

THE FIFTH DREAM

One night just before spring, the Scribe dreamed that he was seated beside a river. It was the first day of the world and although it was not his to possess, the Scribe believed it was his to record. So he determined to make a perfect copy of creation. Pen and ink were ready on the page of sand and he was poised to copy the river down.

Awestruck, he gazed about him, breathing roses; wonderstruck, he listened. He saw the sweet gazelles dipping softly in the stream, raising almond eyes in the green gloom. He heard the azure birdsong concealed by mist among the immemorial trees. He sensed the evidence of emerald gardens glimmering high above the rocks, the testimony of the tree that leaned across the river, the proof of the sheltering bough in the musk-laden air. And he knew that what was true then could be true for ever as long as he made a faithful copy of it.

But the river was flowing too fast for him to write it down. It flowed fierce and cold across the page of burnished gold; it escaped between the crisp stones of the words, curled down the mountain and pounced like a silver fish. It was alive. And though he bent low and knelt down beside it at the end of his day's work, though he dipped his reed in it repeatedly and attempted to write across that bright translucence, he failed to catch creation in his net of ink. Each time his pen tip touched the stream, it tarnished. Each time he tried to write, it turned opaque. To his dismay the paper tore under his pen, his ink darkened the water and the book of creation was sullied by his copying. It was as though the very flies that buzzed about his head anticipated pride. And it was too late to salvage the page.

Silver tarnishes, he thought sadly, the treacherous silver of the chancery. But he was not one of the palace; his right hand was his only mandate, his thumb his only mark of distinction. White lead was all he could afford, what with the cost of carmine nowadays and the price of gall. Where could he find the albumen to brighten the river of his faith?

I must have used a substitute, thought the Scribe, for the Widow guarded each egg as if it held the promise of resurrection. Yes, he had used cheap gum to bind the white lead pigment. There was something in this recollection that struck him as faintly reprehensible. It congealed the river waters; it thickened the translucence of creation, rendering ripples sluggish under a dull surface. Grief gathered like cherry gum in his throat. Perhaps I have forgotten the art of copying, thought the Scribe. For there was no doubt now that the river was tarnished black. As he stretched out his hand to cup the waters, the Scribe saw his palm was streaked with ink, his hand was scored with a thousand lines.

My hand is my undoing, thought the Scribe. Who can write with a written hand?

The Scribe saw then that it was dusk and the last day of his life and he began to weep. And the tears flowed from his eyes and became a river. And the river ran bright and clear and rippled across the stones. It dazzled like silver across the sands of gold and wiped away the streaks of ink, washed away the writing, marbled the page with argent clouds. And he saw with wonder that a tree was growing from his palm, leaning its sheltering branch across the river. And a thousand birds, scarlet and turquoise and saffron yellow, sang in the immemorial branches of the tree, and a soft gazelle stood dappled in the emerald mist beneath, and listened.

And as the waters leaped towards the new day, he saw another scribe approaching, another scribe walking beside the river that flowed from the palm of his hand. He was bending down at the end of his day's work; he was about to dip his reed in that river. And the Scribe warned him, 'What is true now was true before and shall be true as long as we remember it.' But it was too late. Awestruck, he died in his dream then, breathing roses.

Between the compass points of paper lies the proof of a scribe's capacity.

Between his work's perfection and its defects lies the scope of his intent.

19 SPRING

T he Mullah did not die that winter. Although he drew close to those great gates which took in the venal and the venerable alike, he did not pass through them immediately. Instead, he completed his will. And the way he finished that labyrinthine work was almost as good as dying. For it was a testimony to those who disappeared before him.

The first to go was the Daughter of the Warden.

It was at the turning of the New Year. The spring rains had been heavy and the melting ice on the high passes turned the river to a torrent. The town seemed on the verge of sliding down the mountain in heaps of mud, and the mosque perched above the southern gates tilted precariously. But the equilibrium of power had already toppled in the palace, for as avalanches roared in the heights, and the ice broke on the river, the Warden's Mother had announced that she was leaving and taking her Granddaughter with her. The wedding of the Warden's Daughter and the son of the Khan of the Western Marches was to take place on the eve of the spring festivals, at the most auspicious season of the year, and Her Ladyship was taking her Granddaughter and her dowry over the passes. Several pack animals were loaded with blotting paper which the Charlatan had advised be used as a substitute for wedding sheets but the girl's embroidery box was not included in her trousseau. When the Warden's Mother discovered the illicit hand mirror inside, she paid a courier handsomely to return the wretched gift to the Crown Prince, in a definitive annulment of the royal nuptials.

The Warden had tried to remonstrate with his Mother, to assure her that the betrothal had been annulled long since. He even confessed the dreadful truth to her about his transfer of troops to the Prince. But she was deaf to his explanations. She shut her ears to him and closed her mouth like a lizard until she was ready to leave. And then, she heaved her shrieking peacocks into the litter, cursed him with the paper pox and left him to the Kurds.

But the rains had been so severe, and the melting snows so unrestrained for several weeks, that she did not go far. For the river had broken its banks that morning and the grey waters swept the stone bridge before them, just as the Warden's Daughter and her mule train were crossing over. The parapets buckled under her weight, the stone arches cracked beneath her in a burst of thunder. And the guards pulled back aghast in the tempestuous rain, as horses and mules fell pell-mell into the foaming rocks. They watched in horror as the vast bulk of the Warden's Daughter tumbled into the swirling waters. And the Warden's Mother, sitting in her litter at the bridgehead with two lamenting peacocks pressed against her breasts, stared in mute disbelief at the dwindling figure, bobbing and heaving, rising and falling on the swell of the flood, like a bloated bladder filled with yoghurt. She disappeared from sight several times only to reappear again among the distant rocks in the most undignified postures and unvirginal positions. At one point she waved happily at people gathered on the riverbanks, seemingly unperturbed by their cries and desperate shouts as they tried to keep up with her relentless progress. They saw her riding the crest of the curving river, perfectly poised for several moments, and then her massive prow turned slowly and capsized into the froth for ever. When that smooth orb slid beneath the glittering waters for the last time, the Warden's Mother pursed her lips and ordered the entourage to plod on. But she died of a broken heart before she reached the Western Marches.

The torrential rains did not cease all that day and the river was soon impassable. Several donkeys were retrieved, braying mournfully in the flooded orchards; saddlebags were festooned like forgotten laundry among the budding fruit trees and strewn about the muddy cotton fields; a soldier was also swept away in an attempt to snatch some silken cloth caught in the rocks which proved to be a sodden bolster, but there was no sign of the girl. The following day the desperate search continued, but the body of the Warden's Daughter was never discovered. A silken slipper filled with cherry blossoms was fished out of the water; quantities of paper pulp were untangled from the reeds; dozens of goats were mourned and a bloated beggar was discovered face down in the cornfields, but that immense body simply disappeared. She seemed to have melted into thin air. Peasants in the fields as far away as Khoy reported hearing high laughter on the day of the flood. Some said the poplar trees all the way to Tabriz fluttered with her pale undergarments and others swore they had glimpsed a moonlike face under the surface of the southern Salt Lake. But though the riverbanks and ebbing pastures were searched for weeks afterwards, though the waters of the river Aras and its tributaries tasted sweet throughout that spring, the girl was never seen by anyone again. Most people believed she had drowned herself to escape from the tyranny of marriage, and celebrated her virgin freedom in spring festivals from that time on.

The Crown Prince too was haunted by the Warden's Daughter. As his subsequent marriages proved, he was fated to yearn for fat, provincial maidens ever after, especially those endowed with thick brows and downy upper lips. According to one story, he caught a glimpse of his ill-fated, would-be bride's reflected face intact within the oval hand mirror which was returned to him, and was so smitten by her beauty that he cancelled his demands for Kurdish troops immediately. According to another, he glimpsed her naked body gliding slowly beneath him as he crossed the river at Julfa, on his way to the northern garrisons, and was so shaken by the sight that he came close to abdicating his powers. He was destined to be afflicted with this unsettling of equilibrium on two other occasions. The first was when he faced regicides soon after his accession to the throne, who aimed at him with bird shot and missed. The second occurred in his hall of mirrors when he received news of a victorious battle just as his son died of a fever. According to a third legend, the unveiled features of a woman deprived him of his senses four decades later too, when he was finally assassinated. It was as if he was doomed forever after to contemplate the futility of his achievements in the face of the colossal inaccessibility of the Warden's Daughter.

As for the Russian, he left town in the wake of the hysteria caused by the advent of the Crown Prince. One of the winter couriers claimed that brigands had dispatched the young man over a precipice long before he ever reached Tabriz, for shattered femurs were found among the gleaming compasses and mirror fragments at the bottom of the passes in the melting snows of spring. But in most people's opinions, a man who could walk out of the burning embers of the coffeehouse unscathed could easily survive the onslaught of mountain robbers. He rose from ignominy, according to the gossip, and was granted high distinctions when he returned to the capital. His official report delivered to the Russian Minister was described as a tour de force of political diplomacy, shrewd judgement and prophetic insight. But although this remarkable document was destined to change the map of empires for ever, it was never positively identified by later historians and its fate was finally as uncertain as its author's. For the only trace of the young man's exploits, discovered years later in the archives of the Winter Palace by an inquisitive cousin, was a lacquered writing box of feminine dimensions that contained five starched collars, some maps, a talismanic button and a pair of cuff-links.

The Minister's daughter married a count on her return to St Petersburg.

Soon after the disappearance of the Russian and the death of the Warden's Daughter, the Prisoner also departed from the region. Letters had been coming from the Prime Minister since early spring, accusing the Warden of laxity. The Russian Minister had apparently brought pressure to bear on the gouty Shah regarding the activities of the notorious prisoners placed under the Warden's custody on the north-western borders. It was rumoured that documents written by one of them had been delivered into his hands which purportedly threatened the Qajar throne and contained dangerous prophecies about uprisings among the Turkmen. Some even thought it was the Russian agent who had delivered these; others claimed his report was a mere copy of them. But since revolutions had been caused by reasons even less original during that catastrophic year, it was understandable that the Russian Minister would want the author of these subversive papers to be removed as far as possible from his country's borders. It was believed that he used the occasion to score a diplomatic advantage over his English counterpart and to shift the balance of foreign powers in the region.

When he heard of this story, the Mullah did not know what to believe. No one could tell him for sure whether these papers concerned current occurrences, future happenings, or were a record of past events. They were variously described as containing a prophecy and simultaneously its fulfilment, a threat of insurrection and a prayer for protection, a simple manual for scribes and a meditation on the futility of writing. According to some readers the document was a laissez-passer; according to others it was a testament. A few thought it was a poem, though most averred that the calligraphy was derivative and indicated a poor copyist. Certain persons were of the opinion that it contained badly rendered miniatures or maps torn from their bindings and separated from the texts they were intended to illustrate. And the most malicious gossip was that the document was entirely blank: one eyewitness swore that it contained nothing at all. The only fact on which all these theories converged was that the paper of this document was green: as green as the first blades of grass on the bare slopes of spring, green as pistachios, and a goat's insouciant eyes.

They said the Warden lost his authority in the region because of these green pages. His behaviour had become increasingly erratic in the course of that year and he was subject to savage somnambulism, according to the servants.

It was rumoured that from little sleep and much suspicion his brain was wiped blank and his judgement erased. All through the winter months he dreamed his nights away across the frozen countryside and by the time the Kurds raided that spring, he was fast asleep all day. One dawn, soon after his Daughter's demise, he was found somnambulating down at the bridge accompanied by a pair of his best stallions. He was apparently there to greet the newly arrived chancery secretaries who were the Prime Minister's spies, though it was also possible that he had gone to arrest two poor scholars who had walked the length of Persia to bring more supplies of paper to the citadel. But one of the guards at the toll bridge stated that in his opinion His Honour had been written down there by the Prisoner. The Prisoner could write anyone where he willed, he averred solemnly, and the Warden was a pawn in his hands. It was hardly surprising, therefore, that the Khan was relieved of his duties and compelled to relinquish his garrisons to his half-brother. Shortly afterwards, the Prisoner was sent to a fortress further south, under the strict surveillance of another warden notorious for his ruthlessness, and the Khan disappeared from the region.

The Mullah witnessed the disappearance of the Russian, the demise of the Warden's Daughter, the departure of her Grandmother, and the downfall of the Warden. But although he survived the winter himself, he was forced to part with the Widow too.

Some days after the flood bore the Warden's Daughter away, the Mullah called for a feast in honour of Noah. He wanted to be reminded of covenants, whether or not there was any hope of their being renewed. Although the old world had been lost, he wanted to contemplate a new one pitching on Mount Ararat. The vernal equinox had metamorphosed into a funeral feast that year and theological questions among the townsfolk had become routine. Why had the Warden's Daughter survived the previous winter if she was to be drowned by spring? Were the Kurds instruments of God's wrath, tools of a mother's vengeance, or creatures of habit when they raided the town? Even the women's quarters up at the Warden's mansion seethed with metaphysics. And the Mullah found no answer in his glossary to these quandaries. Since the oblivion of food was his only ballast to spiritual vertigo he determined to resolve these dubious questions in one apocalyptic attack of gout.

The Sufi who had arrived the previous summer was to depart from the region soon and so the Widow decided to adorn the golden splendour of her rice with the five spring herbs, in honour of the season. Despite the recent tragedy at the bridge, her spirits were cheered by the new sprouts of the coming year, by the hyacinth fragrance of the old. She had dreamed the previous night that the verdant basil could not be contained in its pot and had rolled like a green carpet down the mountain and across the valleys of Persia. As if in fulfilment of this prophecy, cooing turtledoves had made their nests in her chicken coop and the Mullah's goat too was flaunting a bloated belly and bursting teats. So, buoyed by signs of life, she decided to barter all her eggs in exchange for the Mullah's favourite cakes of wax and honey boiled together the Turkmen way. For nothing should be withheld when the season was so generous. God was the Limitless, the Outrageous, the Breaker of every Rule, she said.

She hoped the Scribe would buy the cakes for her from the market, for his legs were younger than hers, even if his hand had been afflicted. Since her rice was almost ready and the hour already late, she clattered off in great haste to the stables to collect her precious eggs from the high warm straw, leaving the Mullah seated on the courtyard rug beneath the fig tree, in the company of the Sufi. The rain had finally stopped and although the spring air was damp and chill, a brazier had been brought out of the building for their benefit, and the coals glowing under the Widow's cooking pot warmed them in the last rays of the watery sun.

The Mullah was feeling voluble after the flood. 'You must admit, sir,' he wheezed complacently, 'that God's justice is inscrutable.'

'His mercy is too,' beamed the other.

The Sufi had proven to be the hopeful sort and his simplicities were encouragingly predictable. The old man carried a mirror in his heart, like the Khazar heretics, which showed people what they wanted to see. Only on one occasion had he surprised the Mullah. He had submitted blank sheets of paper to the Warden as petitions to deliver his supplies to the citadel. One of these papers had circulated in the coffeehouse, causing much gossip.

The Mullah sighed. 'But a young girl is drowned!' he protested. 'What kind of mercy is that?'

'She was at least delivered without any lingering maladies,' offered the Sufi.

'Life is one long eructation, my dear fellow!' interrupted the Mullah, puffing hard.

'Although they do say she had peculiar dreams,' continued the Sufi thoughtfully.

'Our worst illusions occur at the hour of our greatest trials,' pronounced the Mullah pompously. 'That's why I suffer from gout after a good meal, dear fellow. But tell me, in your opinion was it God's mercy or His justice that she died?'

'Perhaps the choice is His?' said the Sufi humbly.

'So what's our role in the affair?' rejoined the Mullah in astonishment. 'We must make some attempt at literacy, surely?'

'We provide Him with the best paper possible, sir,' replied the Sufi simply.

The Mullah stared at his guest in horror. 'You don't support the wretched doctrine of determinism, I hope?' he said loftily.

But the Sufi was saved from heresy by a sudden cracking in the stables and an accompanying thud. The ladder had fallen down as usual. The goat set up a loud bleating but, other than the clucking of chickens in response, the Widow's farewell to her unborn chicks was peaceful and protracted, and served merely to distract the Mullah from divine conundrums. The evening breeze stirred in the arms of the newly adorned fig tree; the last rays of a green sun shone through its pale transparent leaves. The rice pot hissed softly on the brazier and a fragrance of saffron filled the air. A small, dun-coloured bird, perched on the branches above the Mullah's head, began to sing, piercingly sweet, as the twilight fell. He was suffused with calm in contemplation of the emerging stars. He sensed the melting breath of spring in the air. He allowed himself to consider that there might be other levels of equilibrium spinning unseen around him, layering the universe in silence. Was it possible, he thought, was it conceivable that somewhere, far below them in the violet-shrouded valley through which the river Aras flowed, the body of the Warden's Daughter floating face down among the river reeds was surrounded by the undiscovered immensity of God's mercy?

As he prepared to launch upon another codicil, footsteps approached up the gravel slope and the dim figure of the

223

Scribe appeared. But it was not until the fragrance of saffron had turned to a distinctive odour of burned rice in the course of the ensuing hour that it suddenly occurred to the three men in the courtyard that the Widow might have changed her mind about selling her eggs. She had gone into the stables before sundown and the horns at the gates were announcing their closure. It was too late to buy the honey cakes.

The Mullah never forgave himself that desire for honey cakes rather than concern for the Widow finally caused him to investigate her disappearance. The old woman had fallen off the ladder and had been lying silent for the last hour in the semi-darkness of the stables, breathing hoarsely. Her frail body was spread-eagled when they found her, the bony hip caught awkwardly on the rough floor. The hens pecked and crooned companionably in the immodest angles of her limbs and the treacherous goat had begun to lick the smashed eggs from among the thin strands of her frail hennaed hair.

At first they thought that the ladder had given way beneath her and sent her crashing to the beaten earth. The distance was not far but her bones were brittle and it seemed that she was broken inside. A trickle of blood curled from her mouth into the Turkmen tattoo on her chin. But it may simply have been the feebleness of age that had caught up with her and laid her low with a single stroke, just when she was stretching towards the ultimate sacrifice. She was deprived of all speech and movement, save that in her right hand, which twitched helplessly from time to time. Since she had always been deaf and her tongue was now stilled, there was nothing left to read but the eloquent creases of her face. The Mullah had never guessed till then how tight her suffering jaws were shut against complaint. She moaned a little when the Scribe tried to lift her but her eyes overflowed with joy when he carried her into the Mullah's room and laid her on the layers of the will that covered the floor. The blood soaked the paper quickly. She was dying.

The Mullah sat on his haunches through that moonless night and listened to the rise and fall of the Widow's hoarse breathing. As the rattle worsened, he realized what a heresy it had been to take her for granted all his life and finally began to weep. He had placed his faith in doubt and never questioned his uncertainties. As a result he had become a devout sceptic, a worshipper of the Unknowable, the Unanswerable and the Continuous Quibble, and lost the opportunity to love another human being. As he stumbled between the gaps of her breathing and fell into the small hours of her silences, he read the Widow's faith inscribed across the remaining pages of his will. It refuted every regulation of syntax and illustrated the exception to every rule. It sang its unspeakable proofs between each line of her life. It showed him how red was the love of God, how real and how unreadable, and his doubts dissolved in its simplicity as he bowed his head before the Most Ancient Heresy of All.

By dawn the old woman was dead, and when he opened the door of his room the Mullah gazed out with washed eyes at the world beyond, as if it were the first day of creation. He noted the nodding poplars knee-deep along the banks of the river Aras. He heard a flutter of doves' wings under the stable rafters. He glimpsed the distant covenant of the mountain graced by snow. And he saw the eastern peaks tinted with the generous expectation of sunrise. The citadel walls, blooming on the bare western slopes, responded like roses. He felt awestruck by the privilege of dawn, even if it was only a copy of the original.

* * *

The last to leave was the Scribe. And he left as silently as he had come, although it was evident that he would not exercise his profession wherever he might go afterwards. This was not only because of the closing of the workshops and the erosion of the manuscript tradition. It was not only due to the demise of the scribal arts throughout the land. Even though the scientific paper of the new dispensation, according to the Charlatan, could be harvested each autumn and grow fresh again each spring, even though it contained a thousand and one words embedded in its chain lines which rendered irrelevant all future copyists, the Scribe's disappearance was caused by far stranger miracles and catastrophes than these.

For in the last days of the Warden's despotic rule, the Scribe suffered a terrible punishment. Soon after the new secretaries were installed up at the palace and an inventory was made of supplies at the chancery, he was accused of theft and subjected to the law of larceny. It was said he had been pilfering paper for his private purposes. Rumours were rife regarding the Warden's wrath. It was just after the death of his Daughter, when his Mother had gone. Couriers were arriving daily from the capital with instructions for the removal of the Prisoner and the displacement of troops. And at the height of the crisis, when the first Kurdish raids began, the Scribe was suddenly summoned up the hill and arraigned for stealing. When he stumbled back to town, he was in a fever that lasted until the Prisoner's departure at the end of spring. The Mullah cared for the poor sufferer, they said, as though he were his own son. His right hand had been cut off at the wrist joint and brutally cauterized.

In most people's opinion, this cruelty was the final proof of the Warden's madness. For the punishment had been inflicted in violation of all the religious regulations. To begin with, paper was subject to easy decay, so why should so lowly a theft warrant such extreme punishment? Secondly, if he had stolen paper in order to waste or destroy it, his act might be considered lawful in and of itself. Thirdly, if amputation need not be incurred for the stealing of a book, then it should not have been inflicted for the theft of such a piece of public property as blank paper either. Fourthly, a paper thief was surely no more guilty than the stealer of a lute or drum, for only an empty mind can find idle amusement on the empty page. And finally, it was most unorthodox, in the absence of all witnesses, to cut off the hand of a man who had merely stolen from a prisoner and a heretic, for the rights of the latter were surely less than those of a dog or a free-born infant, according to the laws of the Holy Book.

But although he never contradicted public opinion on the matter, the Mullah suspected that this terrible punishment had little to do with any law. He was not certain either that the Warden was to blame for such an act of gratuitous brutality. He was not even sure that the mutilation of the Scribe's right hand was due to theft. The latter refused to speak about the circumstances that had led to his having a stump for a hand, like the beggar who used to sit at the coffeehouse door. He maintained an enigmatic silence in the face of all the Mullah's questions and sank into his sickness with a strange relief as though his condition spoke for itself. The old cleric could only ponder the mysteries implicit in his silence.

And as he nursed the Scribe through his delirium in the days that followed, the Mullah noticed a curious change in him. There was an odd light in his features, which bore little relationship to the burning of his cheeks or the fire on his forehead, which extended beyond the exemplary fortitude with which he suffered from his pain. His skin grew pale and luminous, stretched taut as parchment across his bones; he seemed incandescent as if blazing from within. And there was a resignation in him that was neither passive nor embittered but rather expectant, eager for the giving, green with the desire for living. His lips too moved continuously. The old man, bending low to listen, could not make out any distinguishable words in his whispers. But during the night these murmurs filled the mosque like running water, like amorous moans. And at dawn, when the fever lifted, he gazed about him with a light air, like a leaf riding the untrammelled breeze, like a blind man reading the wind. But he grew heavy again in the course of the day and sank beneath recurring fevers each night.

For some time he battled against the onslaught of the infection and then, one morning, early, he woke from a dream. It was dawn and he lay in his reed mat, drenched with the dew of healing. In his dream he had been walking in the melting snow beside a river. He had crossed a chanting bridge and found himself in an orchard on the other side. And then he had seated himself beneath a flowering cherry tree whose leaves were inscribed with the silences of poetry, his butchered right hand hidden in the silk sleeve of his tunic, his left hand resting, palm open, on his silken knee. And he had waited for paper to fall down to him from the branches. He waited patiently and radiantly until the jingling of camel bells woke him.

A camel train was leaving the eastern gates of the town,

on its way through the violet mountain ridges of Persia. A caravan was departing, loaded with luminous paper, perhaps. In his dawning consciousness, the Scribe heard the tinkle of bells and the call of the camel drivers with a wonder bordering on new depths of delirium. But the fever had broken and he could distinguish other sounds now, from the road in the valley below the mosque. He could hear the tramp of marching feet, on rubble and stone, the harsh orders of an armed officer. A retinue of camels and a regiment of soldiers were conducting the Prisoner away from the citadel.

He knew then that it was time to leave.

His room was dim for dawn had barely broken. There was no time to lose and he had little energy to waste. He rose from his mats and found his writing desk already folded and his morning prayers implicit in the blank page of his departure. He staggered slightly when he stepped out of the mosque; he was as weak as a plucked leaf turning down the steep path. But had the Mullah seen the translucence of his face as he hurried after the departing caravan, he would have understood that the Scribe had penetrated past the need for words.

He left no traces in the dust as he followed his new master.

PAPER CHRONOLOGY

The First Millennium

AD 105 In the reign of Ho Ti, during the Chien-ch'u period, the eunuch Ts'ai Lun makes paper for the first time, of mulberry bark. He is appointed privy councillor and honoured for his services by the Emperor and the art of paper-making is decreed to be a valuable state secret, to be revealed to enemies on pain of death.

In the fourth year of the reign of Emperor Yüan Ch'u, scholars are ordered to correct the history books according to the rules adopted by the Han Dynasty. The inventor of paper, the eunuch Ts'ai Lun, is placed in charge of this critical work. He also receives a secret order from the Empress at this time to invent certain slanders and erase certain names in the history he records.

When the new Emperor comes to power, Ts'ai Lun is ordered to give himself up to the Ministers of Justice and be judged for historical forgery. It is recorded by the historian Fan Yeh that the eunuch was filled with such remorse and shame that he bathed and dressed himself in his most elaborate robes, and then drank poison.

445 The historian Fan Yeh dies. His retrospective summary about palace eunuchs, the *History of the Later or Eastern Han Dynasty*, compiled over three hundred years after the demise of Ts'ai Lun, is the first written record of the invention of paper.

700 The Sasanians of ancient Persia import Chinese paper for their state documents but still do not know how to make it. The secret is introduced in Japan, however, where improvements are gradually effected with mitsumata and gampi barks.

751 The 'Abbasid governor of Khorasan sends his lieutenant Ziyad ibn Salih to fight two Turkish chieftains who received Chinese support to rebel against the Moslems. Several of the Chinese soldiers are taken prisoner at the battle of Aslah where they are either forced to give up the secrets of papermaking to obtain their freedom or choose to do so in order to save their lives. In either case they never return to China, and the paper industry that flourished on the banks of the river Taraz in Samarkand from that time depends on linen, hemp and China grass.

The Persian papermakers in Samarkand invent a paper sizing made of wheat starch and the boiled bulbs of asphodel suitable for reed rather than brush pens.

793 The first paper mill is established by Harun-el-Rashid in Baghdad. Thereafter papermaking is exported by the Moslems throughout Syria, Egypt and North Africa.

807 'Flying-money', made of fishnet paper, is recorded in China, and seventy years later Arab travellers to the country note, with amazement, the use of toilet paper.

The Second Millennium

1010 The classic *Book of Kings* is presented by the poet Ferdowsi to Sultan Mahmud of Ghazni, inscribed and illuminated on the finest handmade paper of Samarkand.

1035 The Persian traveller Naser Khosrow is astonished to see that the vegetable sellers in Cairo are provided with paper in which to wrap all their produce.

1127 Roger II of Sicily orders all court documents to be transcribed on parchment because he believes paper has no future.

1140 A Baghdad physician observes desert Bedouins searching the ancient cities of the dead to recover and strip the mummies of their burial cloths, which, when they cannot be worn, are sold to the mills to make paper destined for the food markets.

1147 Jean Montgolfier, imprisoned by the Saracens on the Second Crusade, is forced to hard labour in a Damascus paper mill, from where he returns home to set up a papermaking establishment in Vidalon, between Darmstadt and Mayence/Meinz.

1154 The Moors establish the first Spanish paper mill near Valencia. Despite resistance from the Church, paper begins to be used in Italy instead of parchment.

1221   Paper is banned by Emperor Frederick II, King of Naples and Sicily.

1294   Paper begins to be made in Germany and its use and manufacture spread throughout England and Holland during the next fifty years. Genghis Khan lays waste the workshops in Persia. Paper money is noted by the traveller Marco Polo.

1380   John Wycliff is pronounced a heretic for translating the Bible into English. Italian paper exports dwindle and German mills start up as the Reformation begins to stir.

1400   The Timuri dynasty of Tamerlane spreads across Persia from the river Oxus. The earliest known book printed in movable type is made in Korea.

1455   Gutenberg perfects his technique of typography to block-print the Bible.

1476   William Caxton establishes his printing office in Westminster and the first copy of Chaucer's *Canterbury Tales* is published on English manufactured paper.

1501   The establishment of the great Safavi Empire in Persia which ushers in the golden age of the manuscript tradition. One of the miniatures of this period depicts scribes making paper in a vat, hanging it to dry, before burnishing and sizing it.

1549   Diego de Landa, a Spanish missionary in Yucatan, burns the library of the great Mayan civilization in Manu, stocked with bark paper records from the ninth century.

1550 Marbled or 'cloud' paper, discovered in Anatolia in the previous century, is used by Persian scribes under the rule of Shah Tahmasp, king of the Safavi empire.

1580 The Shah of Persia sends a copy of the *Book of Kings* to Sultan Selim II to sue for peace after defeat. The end of the golden paper age in Persia. The first industrial mills are established in Russia, using hammers and beaters to pound the pulp.

1636 The Great Plague of London is thought to have been caused by scavengers raking the graves for rags with which to make paper.

1666 A decree is issued in England that the dead must be buried in wool, in order to put an end to the threat of future plagues and to save linen for the papermakers.

1676 As trade increases between Christendom and the Islamic countries, the Marti or Financial calendar is created for the convenience of commercial transactions between the east and west, and solar and lunar time finally coincides on paper.

1715 Death of the notorious John Bagford, library thief, book mutilator and the first authority in England on paper.

1720 The first movable type press is established in Istanbul by Ibrahim Muteferrika but the printing industry does not thrive. Although Arabic type was used as early as the fifteenth century, strong resistance to the use of print persists until the nineteenth century, on the part of scribes who cling to the copyist traditions of the old workshops.

1750 The first cloth-backed paper is made in Europe, designed specifically for maps and charts necessary for the expansion of trade, exploration and the profits of empire.

1761 The first forgery of English banknotes occurs, three years before the birth of the inventor of the first paper machine, Nicholas-Louis Robert, in Paris.

1770 Paper is being used to build coaches, sedan chairs, bookcases and screens in Europe. The death penalty is decreed for the copying of English banknotes.

1793 A church is constructed entirely of paper in Hop, Norway. *Papier mâché* soaked in vitriol water is mixed with lime, treated with curdled milk and egg white and then used like plaster. The church can hold 800 and stands for thirty-seven years.

The Paper Crisis of the Nineteenth Century

1800 The first lithographic presses are shipped from Europe to India, Turkey, Persia and Egypt and scribes are employed to write on tablets of wax. Lithography becomes prevalent during the nineteenth century in the Middle East.

1806 The Frenchman Fourdrinier takes out a patent for mass-produced rag paper.

1818 Benjamin Tyler produces a facsimile of the Declaration of Independence for $5 a copy. The 'Rag Trade' is in full swing in the United States and demand is quickly outstripping supply for linen and cotton rags throughout the west.

1819 Sinisen, in Copenhagen, tries to prove the practicality of using beetroot fibre as a substitute for rags in paper-making. Various proposals for alternatives to rag are explored from the 1750s on, including seaweed and wasps' nests.

1825 British ships en route to India include paper among the items traded at Bushire. The Decembrist uprisings in St Petersburg lead to the establishment of the Third Section, Tsar Nicholas's spy network. Coded papers flood the Winter Palace.

1827 The invention of enamelled paper in England, and transparent cellophane paper in New York. Also, *papier linge* in France and silk-thread paper for banknotes.

1828 Persia cedes Aran and Shirvan (later named the Republic of Azerbaijan) to Russia and submits to trade monopolies in the Treaty of Turkmanchay. Paper is imported into the country from Russia and Germany by Greek and Armenian traders, through the northern Trebizond route; British paper reaches Persia en route to India through the southern port of Bushire, in the Persian Gulf.

1837 The renowned poet Pushkin dies in St Petersburg, in a meaningless duel provoked by jealousy aroused by the circulation of blank sheets of paper.

1841 The French scholar Louis Dubeux notes that in Persia babies wear paper scribbled with prayers in their swaddling clothes and beggars appeal for alms on strips of cheap local paper. But by the middle of the century,

Persian scribes become increasingly dependent on imported paper from Germany, Austria, France, Britain and Russia. Hardly any paper is manufactured in the country. As a thousand-year-old tradition, with all its associations, comes to an end in Persia, the first attempt is made in Nova Scotia to create paper from wood pulp.

1844 Samuel Morse demonstrates the first paperless message to Congress, the words 'What hath God wrought?' telegraphed from Washington to Baltimore. One year later the first ground wood paper is made on a commercial scale in Saxony.

French and English newspapers begin to circulate in the Persian court. Presbyterian missionaries from Philadelphia establish a printing press near the salt lake of Urumieh in Persia and begin to print bibles in Nestorian. A paper mill, built by the Russians in the north of the Persian capital, fails abysmally.

1845 Edward Burgess, a young English translator and editor of the first newspaper published in Persia, writes to his brother that although the original manuscripts of the *Book of Kings* could not be bought for less than £100, 'you might perhaps buy a printed one for as many sixpences'. He confirms that printing houses abound in the country and that 'books have become so cheap in Persia that it has done much injury to the trade of copyists'.

1846 The cholera epidemic which began in Bokhara in eastern Turkestan sweeps through St Petersburg, crosses the North Sea and lays siege on London. After passing through Belfast, it leaps over the Atlantic to Staten Island, floats up the Mississippi and finally peters out in Cincinnati in 1848. The deadly spread of the disease is plotted by the press, whose every prediction is followed by fulfilment.

1847 Revolutions erupt across Europe. Pamphlets, tracts, posters, manifestos flood the streets of the capitals. When newspapers finally arrive on the Caribbean island of St Croix, the Negroes revolt against their Danish overlords and demand freedom.

Documents purporting to be prophecies about uprisings among the Turkmen reach the Russian Ambassador in Persia and he insists on the removal of a prisoner accused of heresy from near the Southern Line, as a precautionary measure.

1848 During the economic crisis which paralleled the European revolutions, James Rothschild, defending himself against allegations of the new French regime, writes, 'People think I am made of money, but I only have paper. My fortune and my cash are converted into securities, which at the moment have no value.' The survival of the House of Rothschild is considered 'well-nigh miraculous'.

1850 Valentine cards and personal stationery on 'lace paper' become all the vogue in the west. The first paper bags are invented in the United States.

1855 Egyptian mummies are imported to the United States and thrown into the paper mills in Maine, causing an outbreak of cholera among the rag-pickers, a scandal in the newspapers, and a renewed interest in wood pulp for paper-making.

1866   The first permanently successful telegram connection is made across the Atlantic.

1867   A song entitled 'The Age of Paper' becomes popular in the London music halls, illustrating all the uses made of paper. Paper coffins are constructed in the United States, similar to those made by the Persians over half a century before.

1870   The *Gazette des Tribunaux* in Paris publishes a scandalous article revealing the activities of Vrain-Denis Lucas, Prince of Forgers, who has cheated the manuscript collector M. Chasles of more than 140,000 francs by fraudulent means.

1876   A device is developed and patented by Alexander Graham Bell which can communicate speech carried through wires by an electrical circuit.

1882   The word 'telepathy' is coined by Frederic William Henry Myers.

1889   The Imperial Bank of Iran issues the first paper banknotes in Persian history, stamped with the smiling face of Nasir-id-Din Shah. Subsequent devaluations in the currency do much to undermine the authority of the Qajar dynasty. The assassination of the Shah occurs less than a decade later.

1900   A mendicant Taoist priest discovers a store of rolled paper manuscripts from the first millennium in the Tunhuang caves of Turkestan. Einstein graduates from the

Federal Institute of Technology in Zurich and begins to explore light quanta.

1907   The last handmade paper mills are closed down in the United States, one year after Dreyfus is finally exonerated in France after it is proved that he had been falsely condemned, more than a decade before, on forged evidence.

Towards the Third Millennium

1930   Vannaver Bush builds a differential analyser, capable of storing and retrieving electrically processed data.

1933   Hand-manufactured paper encouraged in China to keep workers employed. Most of the paper produced was used as 'spirit paper' in Chinese religious rites.

1943   Research begins on an 'electronic numerical integrator', ENIAC, the prototype of the modern computer. ENIAC was a megalithic dinosaur, consisting of 19,000 vacuum tubes, 1,500 relays and many thousands of resistors, capacitors and indicators. It devoured almost 200 kilowatts of power, and was capable of plunging a city like San Francisco into a major blackout.

1956   Rank Xerox is established in the UK and the age of mega-copying begins.

1968   Intel is founded. Student uprisings and a vogue for personally rolled cigarettes in thin, 1.5 × 2-inch tissues marks the decade. Kleenex advertises its 'Wet Strength'.

1972 The first fax machine is developed for the US market, raising questions about the legal authenticity of copied signatures.

1980 Increased use of telephones, fax machines and computers encourages the fallacious notion of 'the paper-less office', which multiplies rather than reduces paper use.

1981 The first successful personal computer, IBM PC, is placed on the market.

1990 The emission of greenhouse gases and fear about the destruction of the world's forests lead to heightened environmental consciousness and paper recycling in the last decades of the twentieth century. Recycled paper becomes 'politically correct'.

1995 The Paper Reuse System enables print to be re-moved from paper. Intellectual property rights join the catalogue of human rights that feed the legal profession.

1996 The PalmPilot is invented, followed by wireless access to the Internet. E-mail, e-books, e-pens and e-paper expand the vocabulary of digital e-stationery.

1999 The September earthquake in Taiwan causes a direct loss of $10 million to the Macronix company, Taiwan's largest maker of flash-memory computer chips.

2002 The first edition of Chaucer's *Canterbury Tales*, printed by William Caxton in 1470, is digitalized and made available by the British Library on the Internet.

The Tablet PC, which is only three pounds in weight and small enough to fit into a hand, is placed on the market. The Tablet can transfer handwriting into electronic images, and restores the grace of pen and paper to the art of reading and writing.

The first paper begins to be made with the pulp of genetically modified trees.

A NOTE ON THE TYPE

The text of this book is set in Berling roman, a
modern face designed by K. E. Forsberg between
1951 and 1958. In spite of its youth it does carry the
characteristics of an old face. The serifs are inclined
and blunt, and the g has a straight ear.